AF405574

JANSEY

THE GOSPEL

ACCORDING JESUS' FLESH

© 2022 – Private Publisher
Tulio Jansey Coelho de Franca - Jansey Franca
All rights reserved.
ISBN - 9798848646795

To my wife, my best friend:
Eluenia Franca, thank you for always supporting me.

INDEX

MARY

\- **Escape to Egypt? -** I questioned myself indignantly.

Egypt in our lives again. Egypt seems to have always been in us. It is not only slavery, but purification. Fleeing there is not a simple sentence against our transgressions, but a way to erase them. It is as if everything bad stayed there, and everything good escapes from there. Anyway, sometimes it is like that everywhere: we just want to escape from what happened to us. To bury far away from our gardens what brings us shame.

A few months and this whole picture was unthinkable. Escape to Egypt? Never, because even today it symbolises for all of us a return to the shackles from which we escaped in order to experience the taste of independence. But Egypt symbolises a certain liberation, without which we would not have Moses and the law, even if none of this represents true freedom, mere subterfuges for a bearable existence. In practice we have exchanged the Egyptian chains to bind ourselves to the cords of the law. From where we look our steps are always controlled, our dreams are frustrated.

The freedom we pursue so much is an illusion. We are never really independent. It's like this scenario that seemed to have been mapped out all along. As for me, I have never felt truly free. It may be strange, but I remember everything very well, and I am just an abandoned miracle. I never understood why parents, who could not have children, fast and promise to have them and then abandon them. I believe that God's care begins in the environment in which we are born. Children should not grow up without their parents, especially a daughter, who needs to be taught everything by her mother, to learn to be a woman.

I believe that it is there, where things do not always resemble a true family, that God begins to teach us about life in his own way. Family is not always what we expected, and almost never is. It all depends on whether we are willing to learn the lesson they are teaching us. The imperfections of our parents help us to be better parents. Our trials should only transform us into better and more hopeful people. However, sometimes, some trials tear away all the faith and hope we had. And the worst wounds are those opened by the people we love. They never heal.

I grew up hearing that that choice had been the best for me. And I hated it from the first moment.

Everything might have been entirely different if my parents had grown me up. It's not that I feel wronged. In life, not everything is a matter of fair or unfair, of right and wrong. What I was tasting was only the feeling of a daughter who has gone through situations that could have been avoided. Our stories of faith teach us vividly that not everything always goes well just because we are close to God. When we are under the light it is always easier to observe what we had not noticed before.

It is, therefore, that being educated by priests did not deprive me of the sorrows I faced, nor of having my beauty and innocence stolen. In a macho world a woman's beauty is a commodity of personal pleasure, the hypocrisy of self-denial is false poverty, priestly separation is hidden hedonism. In the end, all are defiled because impurity is not outside man but as part of his nature. Indeed, shamefully we learn that God is a mere concept in the mouths of his representatives, not a way of life. We learn, as I learned, that there is no such thing as holiness, but only the worldly in religious garb.

In that environment I was supposed to consecrate myself and learn more of God, but I was repeatedly abused. I had my soul violated by discrimination, my faith raped by lack of witness, my femininity commercialised. All because in the eyes of the law I was not fragile, I was just inferior. It is the law that deprives you of the right to choose. The same law that teaches us of God, induces us to despise those who are not apparently perfect. In the end the law does not correct, it only judges, and the court that observes it suffers from a completely imperfect bias.

My heart was revolted. I knew the hell of being a Jewish woman and the demons of flesh and bones. In time men started to call their shameful impulses demons. It is much easier to attribute to an external and invisible force a behaviour that we are incapable of justifying. And so I was prevented from crying out my pain, like so many others who similarly knew impurity at the hands of those who should present us with the path of sanctification. We were all promised to men who still saw the sacred in that context, even though we were aware that there was nothing sacred and that in the house of God it was as if he was not there.

Objectively, we were children abandoned under the hypocrisy of a vow. Brought up in the temple and promised to elders or widowers according to the traditional custom. We had no say, no choice, and we all wanted to escape. We were still childish enough to assume any kind of responsibility and when we sought God, wanting a greater spiritual participation that would take us out of that situation, and that he himself would tell us what his will was in our lives, we were recriminated and warned that women were not allowed to do that. And for simple children those words were as if not even God wanted us. What kept us going was no longer the hope for a better future, but the beauty of a promise. No one knows the value of a promise until they don't lose everything. While we have family and support, friends and resources, a promise doesn't mean much. When all is going well, a promise is something beautiful that we believe in but don't care about. However, when we have nothing left but a promise, it becomes the only reason hope exists, and it educates us to believe and trust, for any promise needs time, a time freed from urgency and devoid of price.

That promise of marriage shadowed our pain and nourished hope. We had all received that same promise. A wait that had an appointed date and time, even if they were schedules that manifested differently in each one of us. We had an appointment with sexual maturity and that, when it reached us, we would be redeemed by the one God - or fate - had chosen us for a husband. This period in which we awaited menarche was a mixture of hope and fear. We wanted marriage more to get out of that reality, but without knowing what it was to be a wife.

The only certainty we had was that we would love our children completely and entirely contrary to that of our parents. No vows would separate us from our children, not until they were able to understand how much they were loved. I, on the other hand, had been promised to a much older man and a widower. But from the time Joseph took me on as his responsibility, he never spoke a word to me, he was never present in my afflictions, he never knew that I suffered resignedly, and I never let it show. It is interesting how we are able to conceal suffering under the yoke of oppression.

We had become skilled at pretence. Religious life was in constant decline. It is as if everything was inevitably and tragically connected. For a nation that had never really been free, that from Egypt had faced so many other enemies, and now found itself once again dominated, it was a picture that made even the most spiritual of men lose faith. In the face of such circumstances fear reigns, not the Lord. Because of the law, faith in Israel functions as a brake on human impulses. When faith weakens, everything that the law seeks to prevent becomes violently and maliciously present.

And when suffering and tragedy make us ask where God is, the only thing we find is the worst of ourselves. It is that without God we do not become independent, nor bigger or better. However, only the idea of God draws out the best in us. Man was not born to become divine, and it is when he pursues what he cannot have or be that he loses his own humanity. We do not exist to become something we are not, we have no obligation to change, but only to be what we have always been and manifest our best, just as Moses' compassion convinced God not to kill our ancestors in the desert.

When we dedicate ourselves to being what we really are, we let our virtues flourish, even if they are always accompanied by our defects. The defects exist so that we do not become independent, because it is our imperfections that make us dependent on one another, just as it is our sins that bring us closer to God. The perfect reveals in us only pride and appearance, behaviours that destroy us mutually and which are always more present in spiritual arrogance. To think you are better than you really are is like looking at yourself with eyes full of sand and always having the illusion that you know what you are seeing.

And if life in Israel is still like this today, there is a worse condition than wavering in faith, which is when we lose the will to continue to have hope. And I found myself in this way. I no longer wanted to believe or trust the ancient prophecies. I felt as if I had been dreaming lost dreams all my life, and there is nothing worse than becoming aware that certain things will never happen. My smile no longer hid my tears. Without dreams it is as if the soul is adopted by suffering, and not even the burning desert sun can light up the journey.

Losing the strength to have hope is something beyond despair, it is more than not having hope. It is not wanting to feel hope ever again. When one loses hope it is not that one loses patience or that one gets tired of waiting. Losing the will to hope has nothing to do with time, which we no longer even notice, because it is not that we start doing things today. One simply does not do, one no longer knows what to do, or when to do it, or where to start, or even less why to do it. The only feeling that exists is that nothing will change, no matter what you do or how much faith you have or how much you put into it.

Once hope is lost, one dies inside and dreams are extinguished. I had no reason to nurture any more prospects. My mother would not help me choose my wedding dress, I would not wait for my fiancé at the altar. No wedding party, no wine, no music, no dancing. Nothing. Neither had I fallen in love and neither had the wedding been arranged by my family. It was all strange and empty and I was a woman deprived of her purpose: to be the faithful wife of the man she loves. Once my feelings and my dreams were denied to me, I could not hope for anything better. I couldn't and wouldn't even hope anymore.

The only question I kept asking myself over and over again was how could you love someone you hadn't fallen in love with? Only today do I know that true love, the kind that lasts, is learnt over time. Love is not a feeling that is born violently, but it is the feeling that teaches us to recognise the values of the other, that is perfected with contact. A feeling that I was completely unaware of when God chose Joseph as my spouse. At that time the only feeling I nourished was a kind of despair, since I could not find death.

Despair, in turn, is capable of creating chasms. You always have something to lose, even when you think you have nothing left. Nobody is ever without anything while they are alive. There is always the probability of something different happening, something that brings us deep regret for our inconsequences. I, who was waiting for the day to be handed over to Joseph, was protected in the temple. We all felt safe because, besides being the temple of the Lord, the Roman militia was guarding it from outside. The elders who waited for us as wives, paid the guards to watch and protect us, and there, in an atmosphere dedicated to prayers, the walls looked like fortresses, and we slept heavily.

When late at night, in a nation at war, the guards guarding the walls invade our dormitories, the first thing that assails our thoughts is that they have come to save or protect us, but never that they have come to violate us. The abuse is of such violence that it is known only when it is experienced. Until then we have heard about it, we know what it is, but we never imagine that it can happen to us. And when it happens, when a woman's body is possessed by someone she doesn't love or desire, she doesn't feel as if she is being used, but as if she is being invaded. From that night I no longer sleep, I no longer dream, I no longer cry.

The only dread that coursed through my veins was what Joseph would think on the day I was handed over to him. I had no way of telling him what had happened to me, because in such an environment the blame would always be mine. The word of a woman, abandoned by her parents, raised in a priestly temple, what relevance would it have against the content of the law? So I repeatedly asked God that, if he really existed, he would have the mercy to take back the life he had given me. I no longer wanted it, I did not feel like a miracle, nor did I see my beauty as a gift. Rather, I felt dead, cursed and condemned.

The days were mechanically and unbearably long. I lost count of how many times I attempted against my life, how many times I thought of abandoning myself to emptiness, to madness. During the baths I rubbed stones on my body, wanting to get anything that wasn't Joseph out of me. I walked with my head down trying to hide my shame. Despair, at first, takes refuge in faith, in prayer. But when prayer receives a silent answer, and the days go by, and nothing is renewed or transformed, then despair takes refuge in the shadows, in death, in the desire not to exist.

That night had changed not only who I am, but all of us. It was too heavy a burden that we had sworn to silence. My life, personally, began to improve when Zacharias started his priestly activities. At least I could talk to Elizabeth every day. However, when the child in

Elizabeth's womb leaped out, I recognized that something in me was growing too. And my dilemmas increased. Why me? Why only me? None of the others thought they were pregnant, only me. And why was that? Disoriented, the lie seemed a viable alternative in a world of superstition, and when the clothes no longer hid my belly, I blamed God and said it was yours, your work and your responsibility.

In fact, I didn't want to lose the child. Even if the law found me guilty, the child in me was innocent. Inside, I firmly believed that when I told Joseph that I did not know what had happened and that my pregnancy was a miracle, I had not lied. A miracle depends on who observes it. Two strangers sharing bread for many is not a miracle, but it is for the hungry. I was becoming a teenager, but I was just an abandoned child. In such circumstances anyone would believe anything, even if I later confessed myself to Joseph, demanding from him more than support and understanding.

Still, circumstances developed in such a way that they decided to force me to drink that damned water, and despair, the fear of losing my son, consumed my bones, while my lips drew closer to God and I told him all that I could not hide. Before me was my sin, whether because I was a woman or a Jew, yet it was entirely mine. However, in my tears my mother's devotion was also present. There, in the confusion of that terrible and indescribable picture, I no longer cared about the consequences that would come upon me. It is that when we suffer continuously, death is more than a relief.

My anguish was the torment of not knowing what would happen to my son. He was already all that mattered to me. My legs were missing, my arms were trembling, but I had to trust in the divine plans and in Joseph. After talking it over and deciding, we went to the test clad in false security, thinking that in the worst case scenario we would die together. On my face was a certainty of peace, but in my soul a hellish torment. And while fear embraced me, my prayers were interrupted by a presence, neither human, nor divine, just what was necessary for me, as if time stopped around me.

- **Woman, what are you afraid of?** - that stranger said to me.
- **I am afraid of what will become of the child I am carrying in my womb.** - I answered with a trembling voice.
- **This evidence is a sentence against your life, not against the life of the child.** - Explained the stranger.
- **I'm still afraid. -** I argued.
- **For you or for the child?** - he continued.

- **For the child.** - I replied.
- **I told you that no harm will come to the child.** - rebutted the stranger.
- **But if something happens to me, I who carry the child in my womb, inevitably it will also happen to the child. -** I tried to explain in a soaked voice.
- **However, I told you that nothing will happen to the child, so its bearer will also be safe.** - said the stranger.

I collapsed. It was already impossible for me to hold back my tears, and I burst into sobs. How was such a miracle possible? A miracle that manifested itself only in myself. After all, a miracle is nothing more than the solution of an entirely particular suffering. I had no answer, but I had no more doubts. I endured the ordeal with one hand clutching my belly, my thoughts on God, begging him to preserve the life of that child so that I could be the mother I didn't have, so that I could love him as I had never been loved.

- **May it be according to your supplications.** - The stranger interrupted me.
- **Who are you?** - I asked.
- **Someone in whom you lost faith so long ago, but who never lost faith in you.** - He told me.
- **My Lord! -** I exclaimed in amazement - **Why me? What will become of Joseph? He doesn't deserve any**

injustice! - I asked in anguish, doubts tormented me and I had so much to ask.

- **I told you that nothing will happen to the child.** - He replied.

His voice was reliable, powerful inside me, as if the sound of several thunders echoed inside my chest, but outside no one heard anything, those who clamoured with me to overcome that ordeal did not know what was going on inside me, nor did they have any notion of who I was talking to. But why me? Weren't all the others victims like me? Were they not suffering like me? Why me and not them? When the news reached us, we knew that some had vomited, others had hemorrhaged, some had miscarried. They all drank from that water, while I remained unharmed.

- **You are Mary, perfect mother without your son having been born to you. You have loved him with the desire to be a mother, and not as the fruit of sin. Sin is not always the gesture that is consummated, but the desire that is consummated in gesture. The child growing in your womb today will divide the world into two: before and after him. What is special about him is not divine, it is entirely human. He will be the result of his parents' love. Just as I am appeasing your heart today, I am appeasing the one who will be**

your spouse, who has returned to his house grieved because he also loves you perfectly, and love conquers all, including prejudice. Neither this trial nor any other thing will harm this child, for the day death surrounds him it will be because he has decided that it should be so. The life that springs in him is his by right, neither yours, nor his genitor's, nor your spouse's, nor any priest or law that can deprive him of the simple right to exist. From your experience he will interpret the law, and with the same love he will see in your house, he will love the world. And it will be this particularity of his that will make the difference that will transform the world, for a messiah, Mary, does not need temples, lineage, consanguinity, laws, or gods, but an example to follow, a place to call home. - The stranger told me.

- **I port the saviour in the womb?** - I asked in amazement.

That presence disappeared as it had appeared. From where I was, I could hear the terrifying cries of distress of my friends that disturbed and forced the priests to go up the hill to see what was happening, while I, healthy and sound, felt the strength of that child calming my heart. It should be consecrated, it should be special, it should be Nazarene. Only thus would he remain under my care, close to my lap, in my arms, until he was ready to face his own destiny. In a scenario of complete restlessness, I stood up with the purest calm in my eyes, convinced that the Lord had forgiven me for what had happened.

Beating the dust off my robes, covering my head in respect, that apparent false calm with which I had begun my prayers had disappeared, giving way to an insurmountable peace, to an unshakable security. The priests looked on with strangeness as they came to the aid of my friends. That childish fantasy that had made us invent the "sect of the pure" was now manifested in only one of us. It was something to forget and we had overcome the worst of it.

- **Mary, are you the chosen one?** - Abigea asked.
- **I don't know. What I do know is that I am no longer afraid.** - It was the most sensible answer.
- **Is that you, Mary? Thank God. The Lord is with you!** - exclaimed Susana.

In the days that passed no one else spoke to me. Everyone had a certain fear and disgust in their eyes whenever they looked at me. I did not care. Elizabeth had opened the doors of her home to me, and living with a priest silenced the evil tongues that rushed in, while I devoted myself entirely to my son. After six months, Joseph brought me into the house, but the only sentence he said to me was: "May the will of the Lord be done".

Sharing the same roof with Joseph was the happiest moment of my life after that fateful night. I still washed myself by rubbing something rough on my body, I cried in hiding, I punished myself, but as the belly grew, faith also increased and I overcame my traumas to become the mother that child deserved. In his silence, Joseph had covered me with affection, love and protection, and since we began to live together I knew that I would never be a wife as worthy as the husband who had chosen me.

Over time, however, the tears of guilt for what had happened to me turned to remorse for what I had caused Joseph, and some days I felt even more unclean. In the eyes of the law I was cursed, were it not for divine protection, I would be feeling much more than just remorse. I never asked Joseph and to this day I don't know if the priests forced him to take me as his wife because we had overcome that ordeal, and I honestly think that I never want to know the truth. Looking at him I see a man dedicated to his family, pure of heart and God-fearing, but when I see myself in the mirror I see only a woman unworthy of the blessings he received. This is the effect of the law, a legalism that slowly annihilates us.

Living in that condition appeased and agitated me at the same time. I found myself where I should and wanted to be, but hearing nothing but the necessary words from Joseph to run the house well, caused me strangeness, a feeling of inferiority. It was as if I was his obligation, while he was my ideal of perfect man and love. I was conscious of not deserving him, it was not my undeservingness that mistreated me, for I would accept to live under any condition as long as I could remain by his side. What hurt me was the contempt. I would have preferred a thousand times more his shout, his slap, his look of hatred or sadness, than that look of his on the ground, contemplating emptiness. At the table it was as if his soul was not there. In the nights, almost always spent in sleeplessness, I pretended that, sleeping, I accidentally leaned over his chest, inside his arms, looking for much more safety than pleasure, even because I knew pain, and not yet pleasure. And every time, lovingly he would pull away, letting my head settle on a piece of cloth, and as he rolled my back, hot tears would run down my cheeks, that's when I moaned silently. What I was experiencing wasn't the sadness of feeling rejected, it was the pain of not pleasing him or making him happy.

In a way I knew little of what he was enduring. The absence of a public life did not prevent people from mistreating Joseph's goodness, publicly hurting him with my shame. About this, talking was unnecessary. I just knew every time he passed by the door of his house after a day's work. His countenance was heavy so that it was impossible for me to watch him. My arms wanted to run to embrace him, while my legs chained me to the floor, for if I was the reason for his shame, what good would my arms do him?

- **Mary?** - Joseph called out to me as I turned to my duties at home.
- **Yes, Joseph?** - I replied.
- **Hold me...** - He asked me.

So, as soon as he had finished speaking to me, I was already hanging onto his neck. The pain that had separated us had finally brought us closer together, for it was, at that moment, the only thing we had in common, and for me that was enough. I didn't just hug him. I kissed him, I washed him, I undressed him, I gave myself away. He was all I had and my most precious possession, and at last I was completely his, no longer just his shame.

- **We should take advantage of what happened in Herod's time and flee to Egypt.** - Joseph said to me as we rested.

- **But what about your things, your belongings, everything you inherited from your parents?** - I asked frustrated.

- **Quirino is about to make sense and it is our opportunity so that, on his return, I can register the child in my name. The rest is of no importance. Some of my cousins are in the neighbourhood of Horeb, and we can be there for a few days, and when we return we will move to the region of Galilee, where they don't know us, to give this child a future far from accusations and prejudices.** - He answered me with his gaze full of love.

- **Are you sure about this decision? Joseph, you have already suffered too much, and I don't want to add even more suffering to your life.** - I argued.

- **Mary? Do you love me? After all that has happened to us, I have spent these months watching you, and I have seen your zeal and fear, and I cannot judge you for what has happened, because God has visibly forgiven you. But my question is, do you love me?** - Joseph asked me.

- **Joseph, I will never be able to show you how I feel about you, because while you were faithfully waiting for me, so many disappointments happened to me** that they drowned my soul. **Nevertheless, I love you, for none of that has changed who I am and the promise I received. But how can I show it? I have dedicated myself to you and your family, which today is also mine. My life has been yours, I have waited patiently for your touch, longing for you with every breath. Tell me how can I show you what I feel?** - I answered in distress.

- **You just did it. I recognize in you your sincerity, but I don't understand the reason for so much suffering in our lives, and this pains me, because even if something could be said about it, I don't know if it would serve. Suffering does not bring us any lesson but bitterness.** - He answered me with his voice shaken.

I could only embrace him with my whole body, hold him with my legs, make him feel the child that finally moved in peace and tranquillity, recognizing in Joseph the best father I could wish for. And we became one, mixing our essences.

- **It was great, everything, every moment...** - I replied breathlessly.
- **Forgive me for the times when I explode, for my insecurity, you were all I had left.** - Rejected Joseph.
- **I know that what you have done for me I can never repay you, but what can I do for you? You are special**

in everything you do, a man I can only admire. - I tried to explain, and he was already interrupting me.

- **I don't want you to do anything to me, other than voluntarily feel like mine.** - Joseph said.
- **But I am, Joseph.** - I replied.
- **Mary, I only want that when I leave home to go to work, you hold me as if you were never going to see me again; that when I am at the door and look at you with that look of someone who doesn't want to leave, you look at me with the desire that I should come back soon; that when I go through the door, you throw yourself on my body, desiring me and belonging to me; that every time you look at me, your eyes mist up, let the tears flow, make me see that you don't know how to live without me.** - You tell me, in that way, with that tone, that only I know, that only I have found, that you are entirely mine.

Joseph then planned to leave home, the house that had belonged to his family for several generations. And it hurt me to leave everything behind, because I felt responsible in one way or another for the decision he had to make, even though it was the best for the child, I know how difficult it was for him himself, and this gave me a complete feeling of worthlessness.

To explain his abrupt decision to his children and family, Joseph told them about a dream in which he saw in the sense of Quirino a justification for repeating in Israel what Herod had done years before, and so he had decided to escape to protect me from any act of violence. After discussing our plan, we decided not to sell the properties inherited by Joseph, and to leave them to the children of his first marriage. Anguish consumed me and I always felt guilty. Because of me Joseph was abandoning what he owned, making a deal with his cousins who looked after sheep in Egypt.

I, who only wanted to escape, covering my face out of shame and not fear, was no longer ashamed of anything. What I still felt was the sensation of not having been the woman that Joseph deserved, but that man, with his humble and tired countenance, bowed down to my smallness, and I followed him blindly, trying not to be a greater weight in his life. However, we had no idea when we should travel, what would be the best moment. We were sure that the best time would be at night, because the other acquaintances would not see us fleeing, and would dawn with the surprise of our absence. I had not left the house for two months, the belly could not be hidden, and we tried to avoid new scandals.

- **Mary, we should walk now. Are things ready? -** Joseph woke me up in the middle of the night.
- **Joseph? Why now? It's deep night.** - I answered.
- **Come and see here at the window. Mars shines brighter than any other star. I'm not an astrology whiz, but I don't think it's an ordinary event. The problem is that if I see the brightness of Mars as a sign, everyone else in Israel will have the same impression, and we'd better escape right now.** - He answered me.

When I saw the brightness of Mars in the sky, the child kicked me in the belly, and I hurried with Joseph to leave the house. Abandoning all our other belongings, carrying only a few clothes, Joseph walking to lead two sheep and a cow to provide milk for the child, and me riding the only beast of burden we had, for all the others we had sold to have some money with us, we set out on the road, entirely illuminated by the moon and by that glow that Mars emitted. Just outside the town, the desert was clear. There was no darkness, nothing could hide, and so we decided not to pass through Samaria, and took the road that bordered the dead sea to Bethlehem, where Joseph was born.

That route, although longer than passing through Samaria, would spare us from any nightly rounds which the Roman guards were accustomed to make of the Samaritans, because of the constant conflicts and Hebrew militia, and, passing Jericho, the situation would be calmer. In Bethlehem we could take a short break, eat something with Joseph's relatives, and continue for a few more kilometres to Ein Gedi, but our plans changed suddenly. Passing Jericho, the child started kicking again and the pains became more and more constant. And between Bethlehem and Ephrath, I could bear it no longer.

- **Joseph, I have to stop.** - I said.
- **What happened?** - he asked, worried.
- **I believe it is time and that the child in me wants to see the world. It is a beautiful night.** - I replied breathlessly.
- **I see. Can you hold out a little longer? We're almost in my town.** - Joseph asked me.
- **I don't think so. We need to find somewhere covered and, if possible, help.** - I answered.
- **My father had a property in this area. Near where he brought his flock to eat there was a cave in which my brothers and I had built a small cover to protect ourselves from the rain or the heat. I'll go and check it out.** - He answered as he walked away.

On that clear night, whiter than any other, my son would be born. I knew he would be a beautiful man. The silence was deafening, my legs trembled, and that little donkey had been so good and faithful. At last we would meet: my child and me. Tears streamed down my face as I remembered all that I had endured. When we cross a painful road we fail to notice God's presence beside us, but there, on that empty night, I recognised how close he had always been to me. I believe in a God like that, who turns curses into blessings. A life can never be cursed, and my son would not die because of what had happened to me.

And so we never reach Egypt. In God's plans there are no accidents or chance, this is only the human way of interpreting the divine. Balaam's prophecy was fulfilled in my son so naturally that if it were planned it would not come out exactly like that. God's plans for Jesus were in Israel and not in Egypt, or perhaps it would be better to say that God's plans for Israel were fulfilled in Jesus.

- **I found it! Today there is a family living next door who, unfortunately, have no facilities to take us in, but the cave is there just as I remember it.** - Joseph spoke hurriedly.
- **Then let's go, it doesn't matter as long as we are united. -** I replied.

- **Mary, how strong you are, forgive my distance during these months.** - Joseph said to me.

- **It doesn't matter Joseph, what matters to me is that I am yours, that we are together, that you haven't given up on me! In your distance I loved you in silence, and in your silence I loved you from a distance.** - I explained.

As I straightened up on the donkey, finishing my sentence, Joseph held me in a tender, warm, sweet embrace. And that's how I felt loved for the first time. I wanted to contain myself, but it was impossible. The tears escaped through my mouth.

- **What happened, Mary?** - Joseph asked me, holding me in his arms, trying to understand my weeping.

- **Just hold me tighter!** - I asked, clinging to his neck, rubbing my lips against his beard, smelling his scent and my body pressed against his.

- **Mary, I didn't know I had treated you so badly.** - He told me.

- **Joseph, you did never hurt me. Today I cry because I feel disappearing how much I hurt you.** - I said to him.

- **You never hurt me either, it was not your fault. My anger was with God.** - Joseph answered me.

At this point I was sobbing lost in such a commotion. The doubts, the revolt, the hatred were erased. There, in those thirty meters in which Joseph carried me in his arms, we had the strongest dialogue that we had denied each other in the last fifteen years. The pain had matured me enough for me to see in Joseph everything that not only I needed but that I had always wanted. He was my world and my everything that I had just discovered.

- **Joseph, there has not been a day in which I have not asked myself the same question in prayer. But I want you to know that I have hidden my face and my body out of respect for you, I have never looked another man in the eye out of respect for you, I have never seen another naked out of respect for you. My best days were those when you visited me in the temple. I looked at you from a distance wanting you, knowing that I already belonged to you, even though I did not understand either the motives or the reason for my parents' abandonment. But even though we were prevented from coming closer, inside me I knew that what I would become as a person, a woman and a wife, was an experience that I would like to live only with you. And nothing changed my way of looking at you. Nothing. The only thing different in me is that I started to love you more, I learned to love you, even**

in your silence, in your distance. I understood your pain and admired you even more for having accepted me with such tenderness, living a resigned revolt. I did not hide from my shame, I only wanted to be accepted and to be part of your life, and so I lived the holiness that you deserved, I became the person you desired - I was telling him close to his ear, my voice drowned in tears and pain, when he interrupted me.

- **That's enough! -** Joseph said to me in tears, already bathing my hair - **You are everything and much more than what I dreamed of. -** He finished, with his face close to mine, kissing my forehead.

Comfortably and gently he placed me on the ground. I leaned on a kind of wall that only later I realized was the place where the shepherds gave water to the animals. On the inside of the rock, a cornerstone that protruded from the hill, Joseph improvised a bed with our dresses. The lady who lived in the house next door came to help us, and under a white sky, in that arid desert, surrounded by a few animals, I felt at peace. There, my eyes fixed on Joseph, all the time holding his hand, building the most beautiful love story that the world would avoid knowing, I was confused between smiles and groans.

Inside that small cave, I remember only the prayer I made. Life cannot produce anything bad, for God is life, and my son could not be a curse, a burden or a sin. He was only my son, and the gift of life comes from God. Almost without strength, I, who before was completely unbelieving that anything good could ever happen to me, raised my eyes to that light that irradiated the dark sky of that night, giving my all for that child in whom I had placed all my hope and, thanking God, I prayed:

- **Cast your eyes upon me, turn your face... only thus will I have peace. Turn your face so that I may see you, but above all so that I may be seen by you. Warm me in your arms, show me the right way, make me go on. What am I without you? What can I do without your strong hand? My king, my prince, all my treasure. My eyes chase yours. Find me. Make me your hallowed dwelling place, the place where we meet always, at every moment. Take me in. Only your grace helps me. Discover me, conquer me. I need you. Without you I am straw in the wind, loose thoughts, incomprehensible words. I want you, I desire you, I need you. Come, my only friend. Only by your side do I find reasons to go on.Look at me...**

And as I finished that prayer, my eyes, which were firmly fixed on Joseph's face, slowly lowered towards

Zelomi who was helping us, trying to find out where that cry was coming from. My body completely numb, no strength, but my eyes pursued that cry, until our gazes intertwined. Suddenly, nothing else mattered but welcoming that child in my chest, and I felt that God was looking at me through him, it was as if the whole of heaven was inside that cave.

- **It's a boy, it's a boy! -** exulted Joseph.
- **I know, I always knew... -** I replied almost without strength.
- **What will your name be?** - Joseph asked me.
- **He will be called Jesus, for all that he will do will be divine**. - I replied.

Joseph's cries of joy caused me no wonder. With or without revelation I knew he was a boy and I knew how special he was, and I loved him even without strength. I loved him with every space of that enormous sadness that disappeared from me in a single night. That child, who had just been born, performed the first and greatest of his miracles: to cancel the solitude and sadness that until that night embraced me.

That night, that innocent child had reconciled those I would call father and mother, and erased every year of suffering I had experienced. Joseph took him in his arms as if they were one, as if father and son recognised each other. It may be that this child is the saviour of this corrupted humanity, but Joseph was my personal saviour, and it was impossible not to love him. With him I not only started a family, but had my sins forgiven. Forgiveness manifests itself in many ways when we cleanse our eyes of prejudice. Joseph had washed my soul through his love and his nature.

Those many months, in which I heard the revolt of his jealousy and the self-blame with which he blamed himself for having entrusted me to someone who was untrustworthy, that night were smothered in his broad smile. Before, not every day was a good day, but the good days were capable of erasing all the bad days of the past, and although I knew that once in a while his revolt would be felt, I preferred his company, to endure each day of his storm while waiting for the days of calm. But after Jesus was born, every day was one of calm, of passion and intimacy. Pain and trauma were cancelled, and sewing our marriage was his greatest miracle, it was like turning bitter water into a special wine.

JOSEPH

- Sir, it has become unbearable. It is as if we were shadows. It is as if time passes through us while we remain static, immobile. Nothing changes, nothing is transformed. All we have to do is listen to an old song and tears flood our eyes. We feel rejected, erased, despised. Every day is like walking on shards of ceramic and glass and chewing on nails and thorns. I can no longer bear such indifference. I look around and see people smiling, kissing, existing. I look inside myself and I see ruins, deserts, corpses. It is already beyond abandonment, already beyond a simple ordeal. Nothing but rejection comes to mind. Nothing but sadness comes to my heart. The smile stifles the weeping of the chest. I disguise my complaints by relieving certain mistakes, looking in the opposite direction, ignoring what I cannot change, pretending to be strong. I can no longer bear even my own sins. All the time I wish to flee, to leave, to die? to dust return. It is then that the anguish increases: it seems that not even death wants me. I sit down, play an instrument, rehearse some songs, but my lips say something that my heart doubts. I cannot lie, I have no one to deceive. I praise with insecurity, with fears, with dread. There is the dread of something worse coming upon me. I live attentive, vigilant, neurotic. Rudeness has made my hair white, aged my eyes, marked my skin, traumatised my thoughts. I read and re-read the Valley of Dry Bones, and I resemble those bones, with the difference that my bones are not coming together and neither is my flesh coming to life. I am looking for support, for help, but it is difficult for each one of us to walk alone. If I cannot walk, how can I educate? Who can I help? I have become accustomed to tragedies. Sometimes, at night, I go out a little, I breathe other air, I look at the sky. But I don't look at the stars, I only contemplate the emptiness. It's as if the sky had its windows shut. I would like to jump and scratch these windows that separate me from infinity. But since I am small and the heavens do not open, I cry out but nobody hears me. Those who knew me have already forgotten me. Those who hated me have already relieved me. Those who loved me have abandoned me. Nobody pays any attention to me any more. I venture into some things trying to escape from reality. But when I return, everything is worse. I've become a reproach and people pass me by, shaking their heads. I embrace your law: Who knows something will happen? I reread some old books, I leaf through them. Yet they are only memories, nostalgic memories. Nothingness is the most lasting certainty.

Today I confess my rancour. It is better to be authentic than to hide in facades: Nothing goes right and there is no peace anymore. That's why I give myself up, open book, who knows so I'll have an audience? Run to meet me, come out of your absconding Sanctuary and reach me, I'm on the verge of fainting...

- **Joseph? What happened?** - Mary asked me, interrupting my prayers.

- **For six days we have been in this inn, tomorrow we must take Jesus to present him in the temple and circumcise him, and I don't know how I should grow him, for it is in any case a miracle, a miracle entirely ours!** - I exclaimed.

- **One step at a time, Joseph, because the one most interested in the growth and education of this child is God himself.** - replied Mary.

The days we spent there were good and peaceful. We were far from the accusations and I could see in Mary, for the first time, a woman who no longer thought about her own traumas. So I began to organize our things to go up to Jerusalem and there to present the child. I looked at him worriedly, I was old and I did not know if I would be able to stay at his side until he became a man.

As evening fell, Salome, the other lady who had

helped Zelomi during the birth, came to visit us.

- **Mr Joseph, some men came to ask us if we had seen you.** - said Salome, worried.

- **Are Salome Hebrews? Galileans or Samaritans?** - I asked worriedly.

- **No, they are Persians.** - she replied.

- **Persians!** - I exclaimed in amazement.

- **Yes, and they are rich. They said they came to visit the child.** - affirmed Salome.

- **I don't worry about money, thank God we have everything we need. You said you had seen us?** - I asked.

- **I could not lie or ask them to return from whence they came. They followed the birth from a distance. They said that during the child's birth they heard a heavenly chant, and the light that shone from the cave was intense and white, almost angelic.** - Salome said.

- **But, evident. It was night and all was dark around, of course the light shone in a strange way for those who looked at it from afar. But what might this chant be?** - I asked.

- **Yours, Joseph, when you took Jesus in your arms, you sang something wonderful, saying that this night was different from all others.** - Interrupted Mary.

- **It is just the Passover night text that we traditionally sing as a family celebrating the great deliverance in

Egypt. - I replied.

- **You'd better bring those men here, Salome.** - Anticipated Mary.

- **Right, I'm going right now.** - Answered Salome.

- **Wait. What will we say Mary? We don't even have anything to offer.** - I interrupted.

- **Learn to trust in God, Joseph. Go, Salome, and bring them, please.** - said Mary.

Salome left hurriedly, while I went into the manger to improvise a table or something that would give the atmosphere a domestic aspect and we could thus receive those people. But there was nothing but hay and stones, and the little donkey who, with the cow, was playing with Jesus as if he were taking care of him.

- **You see, Joseph? It's details like that that make all the difference!** - exclaimed Mary.

- **Which ones?** - I asked.

- **Here, now, I see the prophecy of Habakkuk fulfilled.** - Mary answered.

I watched the picture and really, I was reminded not only of Habakkuk, but of Isaiah's words.

- **I understand, Mary. But people don't see the world with your eyes.** - I replied.

- **And even I didn't see it that way, Joseph. He, Jesus,**

has transformed my song. - Mary said.

- **Mary, they are coming closer. -** I told her pointing to three people who were approaching, together with Salome.

- **We come in peace.** - said Baltasar.

- **Welcome in the name of the Lord.** - I answered them.

- **My name is Baltasar, this is Belchior and that is Gaspar. We are part of the Magi, and when we saw the glow of Mars, which was pointing directly at Israel, we knew that something was happening.** - said Baltasar.

- **In what sense "something going on"?** - I asked.

- **Do you know the messianic prophecy?** - Gaspar asked me.

- **Of course, it is a Hebrew prophecy.** - I replied.

- **Wrong, it's a universal prophecy.** - Belchior said.

- **When the prophecy was given to our ancestors, we did not yet exist as peoples, but as a single cell, a single original trunk.** - Gaspar added.

- **It is, therefore, that that prophecy is repeated in all the ancient peoples.** - Baltasar said.

- **Nimrod, Tammuz, Osiris, Mithra, Dionysus, all are types of the same prophecy.** - said Belchior.

- **With the difference that in Israel it was never fulfilled. Just the people who, according to you yourself, would be the heirs of such a promise.** - said Gaspar.

- **So all those gods idolised by the pagans are figures of the same person?** - I asked in astonishment.

- **They are all part of the same prophecy in search of the true sacrifice.** - Baltasar said.
- **Sacrifice?** - Mary questioned.
- **The Messiah is none other than the one who takes upon himself the judgement that God avoids inflicting on the whole of humanity.** - replied Belchior.
- **What do you mean?** - Mary asked.
- **The Messiah dies so that humanity will not be condemned.** - replied Baltasar.

Improbably, Mary's breathing became shallow and she, losing her strength, fainted completely. I, who was listening to everything still not connecting the relationship of the presence of those men to the birth of Jesus, understood the message when I saw the pale despair on Mary's fainting face. The conversation continued for hours as I worried and waited for Mary to wake up. In fact, I could hardly accept what they were telling me, but I had to wait for Mary to rejoin the discussion.

- **So each of those men, those dead gods, was a messiah contextualised in the people to whom they belonged?** - I asked.
- **Yes. Since the prophecy was launched in a remote period for which our antecedents are common, the messianic promise should be presented in the context**

of each faith and culture to which such promise belonged.** - Baltasar explained.

- **And now it is manifested in Israel in the person of our son? But we have David.** - I replied.

- **Your king David, instead of giving his own life, took the life of his enemies. For this reason he was considered unworthy to build the temple, which you believe to be that mountain of stones that is found in Jerusalem, when the prophets of Israel made it clear that you are the dwelling and residence of the Most High, or not? David could not build the temple because his own temple, that is, himself, was contaminated with the blood of other people, or is that not what God told David himself?** - said Belchior, questioning me.

- **Besides, Joseph, this child is not your child. At least not yours. And when he was spared the bitter waters, he also ceased to be Mary's son.** - said Gaspar.

- **It's true, Joseph.** - said Mary, still dizzy, lying on my lap.

- **How? You can't believe this madness, Mary, it's heresy. What will the priests tell us? Rather, what will they do to our son? Do you know how many revolts there are today, and how they are silenced?** - I asked.

- **When we were going through that trial, about to give and lose everything, someone spoke to me, I don't know if in thought or not, but he told me who Jesus would be, and what he is meant to do.** - Mary answered.

- **And that is why we are here today.** - Said Baltasar.

- **But how did you know all this?** - I asked.

- **We have read and interpreted your prophets correctly, and we knew that this child was to be born near Bethlehem, surrounded by two animals.** - Gaspar said.

- **And we are here to take her with us.** - Belchior said.

- **Not at all. No way.** - I shouted.

- **Mary?** - said Baltasar, looking at her firmly.

- **We want to teach you all our arts so that they can assist you in your ministry. We want you to learn to read and interpret the law as we have interpreted it, in the way that has brought us here today.** - Gaspar explained.

- **Tomorrow we must present him at the temple, circumcise him. How shall we do it? This is our chance to register him in my name. It is our miracle, we have just received him. -** I answered, still lost, looking for any excuse to say no to them.

- **You can proceed with all the traditional rites, not least because his name is officially given tomorrow during the circumcision.** - Belchior said.

- **And the next day we set out for Persia.** - Said Baltasar.

- **When he reaches the age of seven, we will bring him back. His studies will continue here, without our presence. By now we will have taught him everything he needs, and the rest will be up to you.** - said Gaspar.

- **But he is a baby, just born. How can you face this
  journey without your mother?** - I asked.
- **Actually, we came in a big caravan, our wives are
  waiting for us in the city, and we have wet nurses for
  that. We came prepared.** - Baltasar said.
- **This is crazy. -** I said, looking at Mary.
- **Joseph, it can't be a coincidence. I don't believe in a
  God who works like that. Look around you, Joseph.
  We know how I conceived him and yet we are here.
  We were going to Egypt, but he wanted to be born at
  the gates of Bethlehem, as in the prophecy. With us
  were only a donkey and a cow, also confirming the
  prophecies. And on the eve of his circumcision, these
  people appear who wish to present him with the most
  important wealth, that is, wisdom. It cannot be a
  coincidence, Joseph. The anguish I carry in my chest
  at that moment is indescribable. My son has just been
  born and I have to say goodbye? To allow him to grow
  up under the care of strangers? Let another mother
  nurse him? How do you think I feel, Joseph?
  However, the destiny of this child does not belong to
  us. I was the only one to become pregnant that night,
  and it cannot be in vain. These are signs that God has
  his eyes not only on this child, but on all Israel. It is
  something bigger than ourselves.** - Mary said, leaving
  me speechless.
- **Mary, I have always believed that a child grows up**

under the care of his parents, within their family context, however, Jesus is more your child than mine, it's your decision. - I answered.

- **Now, I ask you to prepare everything that serves the child. Tomorrow, after the circumcision, we will return to take him with us to Persia, do you agree?** - asked Baltasar.

- **Yes,"** answered Mary, choking voicelessly on the tears streaming down her face.

- **I'm going to call my wife, Mary. This way, you know her. She will grow up Jesus during these seven years.** - Gaspar said.

- **Yes, this time it must be Fatima growing a messiah.** - replied Baltasar.

- **How? How did you say?** - I questioned in amazement.

- **We're older than we look, Joseph. -** replied Belchior, as Gaspar walked away.

- **We exist for the purpose of growing these messiahs who arise from time to time among the ancient peoples, the heirs of the messianic promise. Your child is only the messiah of the present dispensation, but he is also the one who will change the world, because he will represent not only the Hebrews, but all peoples who groan in affliction, who suffer injustice, who need support and help.** - explained Baltasar.

- **In other words, it will rescue what is still human in us.**

- Interrupted Mary.

- **In a way, yes. Mary, this is Fatima, my wife, who is to be Jesus' nanny.** - said Gaspar, coming closer.

I looked at everything with a feeling of impotence, as if there was nothing I could do. I tried not to have an opinion, sitting on a piece of wall, looking at the manger, wondering if I could be the father of that child or if it was anyone who, with the name and the influence he had, was only serving to correct a problem. Fatima and Mary were talking among themselves. Fatima was a beautiful woman, tall, very fair, with a wide, strong body, not overweight, just someone who seemed to have borne more than her own beauty showed.

Anyway, that conversation went on as if everything was settled, and I just thought that we were deciding the future of a person, the destiny of a child, not giving him any choice or alternative. The life he was beginning to know would be the only one he would know.

- **Worried?** - Belchior asked me.

- **And how could I not be? Even though it is not my blood, I always feel a father's responsibility.** - I replied.

- **I know how strange it sounds, but the events that brought about the birth of this child are entirely connected, and were not the work of chance or a** consequence of the choices you made, but of the choices that the Eternal decided.** - Belchior explained.

- **So, do you also believe in God?** - I asked.

- **We all believe, I mean, all peoples. For some it is a force, for others life itself, for the Hebrews a self-conscious being, for us, Magi, God is the one who visited us from the stars, for the Egyptians he is the one who overcomes the eternal conflict of light and darkness, but, in short, who or what is God?** - asked Belchior.

- **He is the creator of all things, the only and sovereign Lord, omnipotent, the Rock of Israel, the Holy One of Jerusalem.** - I answered.

- **No, Joseph, this is just the way in which you understand him or were taught that he would be. Each people construct their own perspective around him. For some he is evil, for others good, but it will always be the same Being interpreted by different observers. The way in which we believe in his existence also determines the way in which he reveals himself in our lives. The interpretation of faith, the study of your law, for example, ends up not becoming an open window through which we can observe God, but a funnel that narrows our vision of him. We cannot imagine him outside that poor conception. So, I ask you, if you were eternal and the direct or indirect agent of life as we know it, would you limit** yourself to being worshipped by a single interpretative form, or would you allow yourself to be found in each and every belief that contained a little truth about you? - Belchior asked me.

- But, a wrong belief in God turns out to be a path of many paths, not a path that leads us to him. - I replied.

- Each and every human idea about God is full of mistakes and successes. And, in fact, more mistakes than successes. However, we always find God through those few right ones in our interpretations. - Belchior explained.

- However, God has shown himself to be strong with Israel throughout history, which means we interpret him correctly. - I grumbled.

- And did not your God himself bless Nebuchadnezzar to correct them? Cicero? And did not your God prophesy through the soothsayer Balaam? It seems, Joseph, that God is more present in our few successes than in our many mistakes. This is his way of presenting himself, because if he depended on a set of beliefs built only on right answers in order to make himself known, he would never be found. Faith in God is not the set of rules that bring us closer to a just life, but the merciful choices that make us understand and help the weaknesses of others, and our own. God is much more the faith to go on when there is no more hope in the heart, than the miracle that changes circumstances. A person who, for example, goes beyond the permitted steps of a Sabbath in order to help a sick person who cries out in pain under the scorching sun of the desert, would be worse than the one who, seeing the sick person, does not help him so as not to break the law? In this case, which of the two has more faith? The one who helps the sick and believes that God will forgive him, or the one who does not help the sick and believes he does not need forgiveness? - asked Belchior.

- It is very difficult, we are brought up to prioritise the law. - I replied.

- Because they have been taught to think only of themselves. However, the law cannot be a justification for indifference. Personal justice must not be an instrument of prejudice or discrimination, but a model to be followed. He who receives the grace to live more worthily should not nurture indifference towards those who have not been able to develop the same values, but should encourage personal improvement. - Belchior said to me.

- I agree with you, however, even if we think so, there are always those who see justice as a mechanism of control and manipulation, and envy and litigate with those who seek to live righteously. - I replied.

- For your law reveals not only what is good, but directly

presents what is evil. The law is not justice that is manifested, but crime that comes to light, because it is the law that says what is wrong while trying to present what is right. Therefore, those who are born deprived of opportunities, unlike you, for example, who come from a rich family, see the law as a justification for the powerful to oppress the less favoured. Therefore, the law ends up favouring inequality, not harmonizing coexistence.** - Belchior explained.

- **However, the law helps us to walk correctly.** - I replied.

- **Yes? Then answer me one thing: which comes first, sin or the law?** - Belchior asked me.

- **The law.** - I replied.

- **No, it is sin. The law was created to regulate relationships weakened by sin, but there would be no law if there were no sin. This means that the law was created after sin, as a way to repair what had been broken.** - Belchior explained.

Belchior's words frightened me, for they presented me with a problem without a solution. Now, if the law no longer served to keep our people in harmony, what use would it be? At the same time, this allowed me to glimpse a little of the road that would be presented to Jesus, and I did not know in what way that child would be able to change the contextualization of the Mosaic law within our culture. In every Hebrew home, in every Hebrew family, in every act of proselytizing, we were taught that divine salvation was our exclusive privilege, and that without the law we could not attain this same salvation. How can we attain salvation without going through the demands of the Mosaic law?

- **Where will he be taken?** - I asked.
- **For Shiraz.** - Gaspar replied.
- **There he will learn what we can teach him. If we are right, at the age of three he will be able to learn much more than any other child of his age.** - said Baltasar.
- **As devastating as it is for me, I'm sure it's for the best, Joseph. I spoke to Fatima and she is already the mother of five children, the eldest being just seven years older than Jesus.** - Mary told me.
- **Mary, I have done everything for you, and I won't go against your decision. -** I answered, while Mary held me by the arm.

The next day we left very early for Jerusalem to present Jesus. We asked Zechariah to perform the ceremony, assisted by Simeon and Caiaphas. There, in front of the community, we officially gave him the name Jesus, much more in the hope that God would protect him than that this name had a prophetic meaning. I took him in my arms, looking into his eyes, not only called him my son, but also recognised him as such. Tears flowed down my face and bathed his forehead as I pressed him close to my face. That was his first baptism and my way of saying that I would always be by his side.

Soon afterwards, on leaving Jerusalem, our paths would part. Mary and I would leave to gather our things in Nazareth and begin life anew in the region of Galilee, while Jesus, protected in the arms of Fatima, would follow his journey to Persia. What he would be taught was unknown to us. But it was as if a part of us was torn away, and precisely the most important part. Strange how we managed to become so strongly attached in such a short time.

- **I agreed to everything, but I have one request to make.** - **I** told Baltasar before they left.
- **And what would it be?** - asked Baltasar.
- **That on the day of the sacrifices for the atonement of Israel, he may be present, together with his family.** - I said.
- **I imagined that would be it.** - retorted Belchior.
- **All right, it will be done like this. It's even better so that you don't show up unaccompanied by the child.** - replied Baltasar.
- **And one more thing. I hope nothing bad happens to

this child, for he is officially my son, and I will spare no effort to avenge his blood. - I told them.

As I walked away, turning my back on them, the three of them left gifts with Mary which, besides being expensive, had a much deeper meaning.

- **These are special gifts, we cannot accept them.** - Mary said to them.
- **I insist that you accept it, it will be useful to you in the future. -** insisted Belchior.
- **But what does that mean, they are paying us for our son?** - Mary asked.
- **No, Mary, they are for Jesus' funeral.** - I answered.
- **What do you mean?** - Mary asked me.
- **The incense for the funeral, the myrrh to embalm his body and the gold to cover the expenses of the wake and the burial. -** I explained.
- **But how dare you insult me like this. He is my son, my son, and I am not giving him up to death. -** cried Mary to them.
- **Death is only a stage in the process of life, Mary. Our intention was not to offend you, but to share your pain. We would only like to contribute not only negatively. Please accept.** - Gaspar said.

That gesture gave me the dimension of the choice

we had embraced, and I took those gifts thinking more of Jesus than of our humiliation. So the days that followed were days of immense uncertainty. We simply did not know if we had made the right decision.

In the first weeks, when we just settled in the Galilee region, we tried to avoid the subject. There, Mary and I were an ordinary couple, even though with the family business my children and I worked throughout Israel. However, in Galilee, far from Nazareth, we were deaf to the hurtful comments that were made about us. People sometimes can't even realize that their own slanders don't make sense. When everything happened with Mary, in the temple I allowed myself to be accused of having touched Mary before her time, while Mary was accused of prostitution and adultery. How could it be possible that I had deflowered her and she, at the same time, had prostituted or adulterated herself? It was an errant argument.

I looked at her tenderly and I saw in her every gesture the desire to do the right thing, and this desire to do the right thing is a model of holiness, it is a stronger witness than repentance. In repentance we recognize the fault for our actions, but Mary, what fault did she have? She was a victim, and when we are victims, a condition arises that we cannot change, because what we did not want happened to us. Here repentance makes no difference, and the desire to get it right is the contradiction between fact and character, just as in Mary.

Her every step was measured, and Mary knew how to transform a simple moment into something special, because she worked with dedication for her family. She knew how to accept the fatality without revolt, and I do not know if my complicity has any relevance, I only know that I could not imagine or wish a better wife in my old age. However, so many things had been silenced between us that the days of friction were inevitable. Most of the time it was useless to try to demonstrate my point of view, always ending up misunderstood and worsening the picture. Therefore, during the years of Jesus' stay in Shiraz, I tried to respect Mary's pain and I tried to withdraw when we argued.

- **I don't know, Joseph, I don't know if it was the best thing we did?** - Mary screamed at me.
- **Mary, this is not what I am talking about, but redemption, a clear conscience.** - I answered.
- **And what do you want me to do? Tell me.** - He kept shouting.
- **Leave it, forget it...** - I answered, walking away.
- **Joseph, I simply do not understand, forgive me. I have**

done everything and also every sacrifice for our good, and if I am guilty before God, I prefer to be guilty for having risked everything for our family and for the future of Israel. - she said to me.

- **What I desire, Mary, is to have a clear conscience. We both took too many risks and I, in my old age, do not want to be blamed either for what we did or for condemning the future of Jesus.** - I was trying to explain.
- **Joseph, this is not the time. Let's talk in another moment.** - She answered me, because the children were arriving for lunch.

In fact, I could tell that she avoided this subject anyway, always giving some excuse. She seemed to want this destiny traced for Jesus to be fulfilled at any cost, either because she believed faithfully in our prophecies and in the interpretations that the Magi had given us, or because it was a way of doing penance for herself. In any case, I was no longer old enough or healthy enough to continue arguing with Mary, and so often I thought that my goodness had caused her to confuse our relationship, as she regularly overstepped her bounds, disrespecting me.

However, I did not measure efforts to see her

happy. At least twice a year I would ask my brother Alphaeus, married to Mary Cleophas, Mary's sister, to accompany her to Shiraz, and when Ioses and the girls, Judith and Ruth, were born, Mary would take them together, allowing Jesus to spend some time with his brothers and sisters and to have some family experience.

Work almost always prevented me from accompanying Mary on these trips, but at least on one of them I tried to be present. However, it pained me too much to realize that Gaspar had a much more fatherly face for Jesus than mine. So, when I visited Shiraz I mingled with the crowd, trying to find out what they were teaching the children, but the secret was always well veiled and strangers had no idea of the content taught by the Magi. Indeed, even to the rest of the Persians it was all a mystery, and only those enrolled in the Magi's school knew what was happening to their intern, and they were vehemently forbidden to spread their voices about the educational process.

What little I was able to observe in our travels is that they possessed medicinal healing techniques that were much more advanced than ours, and used the elements of nature itself, ancient recipes similar to those of Egypt, to modify the nature of certain substances or elements that, for the belief of Israel, were considered magic or spells. They had a rigorous and methodical model of life, as they were local priests of Zoroastrianism, and interpreted the biblical prophecies supported by the knowledge of the stars, to align the events and identify the signs.

- **So, Joseph, what do you think of our town?** - asked Baltasar as he found me by the road, next to the market.
- **It's a beautiful city. I was actually looking to understand a bit of your cult.** - I told him.
- **He must first learn that he is not just a cult, but a model of life. We recognise in Mazda the author of life, the alpha and omega, yet that this life of his has spread throughout the created, and we seek to identify the signs he gives us through this very creation. He is our father, and we are all his children. We relate to him not through a system of rules, but through the devotion of a pure heart.** - explained Baltasar.
- **The heart is deceitful, Jeremiah warned. Our rules serve precisely to weigh our inclinations and discern where the heart is heading.** - I explained.
- **And do you know where your heart leans?** - You asked me
- **Of course it is.** - I replied.
- **Your mistake, Joseph. You only know what the law

tells you is right or wrong, but that doesn't mean that because you know the law your heart inclines only to what is right. What do you do when no one is looking at you? What did your heart and Mary's heart do when she became pregnant with Jesus?** - You asked.

- **What do you mean by that?** - I replied.

- **I want to say that knowing the path of righteousness does not make us righteous. Most of the time it only cloaks us in a false morality. What did Moses do when he killed the Egyptian: did he stay and go through the trial or did he escape? Knowing the law does not make us righteous, quite the contrary, it makes us cunning, as we use the same law to escape its consequences. The knowledge of things does not change who we are. The change only occurs when we know ourselves.** - He answered me.

- **However, without a direction to guide us, how do we know which is the right road to follow?** - I pointed out.

- **All are right and all are wrong. Regardless of the path we take, any road will always give us good and bitter experiences, and both will serve us to know when we got it right and to recognise what we should no longer do.** - He said.

- **And where does this form of knowledge come from?** - I asked.

- **Why do you believe that the law is unrelated to the Egyptian book of the dead? Or that its prophets did** not obtain knowledge when in Babylonian captivity? We who follow Mazda only observe how their knowledge spread and was interpreted among the peoples. - He answered me.

- How is it possible that you know so much about the law and our prophets? - I asked.

- Joseph, and where were your people exiled? Jewish prophecies are a legacy of the Babylonian and Persian exiles, and there we learned much about their beliefs, just as your leaders and prophets learned so much from our beliefs, something they had already absorbed since the great King Solomon. In fact, with the wise king our beliefs began to complement each other. - He answered me.

- We are influenced by masdeism, you mean? - I asked.

- And where do you think Egyptian or Hebrew dualism comes from? - You asked me

- Our faith has no dualisms. - I replied.

- Oh, no? What about angels and demons, or rather, good angels and fallen or evil angels? Law and sin? Even your patriarchs have dualisms, like the chosen Jacob and the rejected Esau. - retorted Baltasar.

- However, our Lord Adonai has no adversary, he is above all as creator. - I replied.

- Yes, and also our God Mazda has no adversaries, but this is because any belief that is based on a sovereign and creative God presumes that this God, who created everything, is capable of destroying it, and therefore that he is above other creatures that were not pre-existent to him. All for the simple reason that theoretically God could not create anything superior to himself. This is the chain of perfection. Something perfect cannot imagine anything better than itself, and therefore all creation is inferior to the creator. - **He** explained.

- **The way you talk it sounds as if we are talking about the same God.** - I told you.

- **And we are not? I thought we were, because if there is only one God, and in every culture or people there is an agreement of this singularity of one God, I think we are all talking about the same God all the time.** - He argued.

- **However, we can also attribute uniqueness to our particular god, which will not make him the true god and will make him diverse in every people or culture. That is, I can take a false god and say that this false god is the true God, when it is not. In this way, we will not be talking about the same God.** - I explained.

- **But, this is a behaviour adopted by all. Hebrews, Egyptians, Canaanites, Babylonians, Persians, each one of these peoples claims that their own god is the true one. Even in Israel, among yourselves, there is the divergence between Samaritans and Hebrews, or Pharisees and Sadducees, or Zealots and Essenes.**

However, the way in which each people or culture understands God is always a personal perspective and part of one's worldview. The way in which God reveals himself, Joseph, is not according to his own nature, but according to the nature and capacity of man to discern and understand. Now, if you were God, creator of all things, would you be concerned about the way in which they believe you or just the fact that they believe you? Do our religious differences matter to God or only to ourselves? Of course, all this discussion of ours has relevance only to the belief system we serve, because our faith also becomes a way of living in society and of governing our society, and God has no correlation with that. Therefore, God reveals himself according to our needs and before what we need from him for our own lives. However, if we then decide to offer to God the sacrifice of children instead of sheep, what is God's responsibility in this? When he required Abraham to sacrifice his own son Isaac, was it not an example that he knows what he wants and provides what he wants for himself, as well as a proof of faith in Abraham's life? Now, if we say that we need to recognize the signs of divine revelation in every culture, but you tell me that the only revelation that exists is the Mosaic law, who is saying this: God or you?** - He continued his explanations.

- **God, for he has given us the law.** - I replied.
- **Not God, you. God gave the law to the Israelites as a way to educate and constitute the people of Israel who, escaping the yoke of slavery, had the need to recognise themselves as a people and nation, under a system of law and beliefs, like all the other surrounding peoples. The law is something specific to the Hebrew people, but it does not mean that it is the only way that God reveals himself in history and reveals himself to other cultures.** - He answered me.

Baltasar's words left me astonished, for there was a reason and perhaps we Hebrews had closed ourselves off to the rest of the world, while God wished to reach everyone.

- **So is that the content Jesus is learning?** - I asked.
- **Not only this. Jesus is learning our medicinal techniques and, with God's help, will perfect them.** - He answered me.
- **It was already a very heavy burden to convert the hearts of our brothers suffering from the oppression of Rome, now it must convince the world to walk in unity. It is even heavier.** - I replied with a sigh.
- **It is the mission of a messiah. All the others before him failed in this purpose, but if he is not able to make humanity walk under the same spiritual**

orientation, he cannot be called saviour, because salvation is a benefit that the messiah offers to all. You see, Joseph, there is no such terminology as "our people" as you have just expressed, except for those who identify themselves racially and believe themselves better than other human beings. This cultural identity has been transformed into a racial identity, but we are not different races. There is only the human race, with particular traits and culture depending on the region in which it develops, but such differentiations should not divide us into other peoples. The Hebrew tradition, which had the purpose of preserving the lineage of patriarchal families in consanguineous marriages, ended up turning into prejudice, and you divided the world into Hebrews and Gentiles, even though we are all human and children of the same God. - He answered me.

Those were harsh words, but true. I preferred to keep silent, for I simply could not argue about something that, even for us Hebrews, had become unbearable. In short, we hid behind a false moralism, which served only as a justification for our omission and indifference.

This year of visitation, the return trip was silent. He had grown up under the care of Gaspar and Fatima, saw us very little and that was hurting Mary, because he no longer called her his mother, while I was a complete stranger to him. However, what tormented my thoughts were the words of Baltasar. As a Hebrew I knew that this kind of message would not please Israel, and if this was what they were teaching Jesus, it would certainly lead to his death. The leadership of Israel would never accept the nature of that speech. Watching him grow, the distance did not prevent me from growing fond of him, and the death of a son is not a project present in the plans of any father, but in our lives it was insistently present since Jesus was born.

- **He doesn't see me as his mother anymore, I don't think he even feels any intense feelings for me.** - Mary said, interrupting my thoughts.

- **Perhaps it's better that way, because if this destiny that you and the Magi have outlined for him really comes true, it will be much better if these ties no longer exist in your life or in his.** - I answered gruffly.

- **But what do you have to answer me so coldly?** - retorted Mary.

- **You're right, I'm sorry. I'm sure he knows you're his mother, but the distance and the situation get in the way.** - I cut the conversation short, not wanting to show my feelings for Jesus.

In the years that followed, preceding Jesus'

return from Persia, I no longer accompanied Mary on her visiting trips, trying to distance myself either from the decisions chosen by the Magi and Mary, or from the fatherly feelings she showed for Jesus. My eyes were not ready to see a child suffer and even less die. I had already suffered enough and, at an advanced age, I tried to transfer the family activity to my children and distance myself from situations that could cause me discomfort. When time passes and we realize that death is an inevitable encounter, we realize how foolish and futile the things we pursue in this life are, and the only wealth we can conquer is peace. Thus, one day Gaspar's eldest son knocked on our door, accompanied by Jesus. Seven years had passed and I, busy being useful and distant from Mary's choices for her son, had not noticed the passage of the last three years. After exchanging a few words with Mary, he came to speak to me while I was sitting in the kitchen.

- **Gaspar's son is leaving, aren't you going to say goodbye? - he** asked me.
- **No,** - I answered.
- **You have not come to visit me in the last three years, why?** - you asked me.
- **I was too busy with things at home.** - I replied.
- **Will you teach me to be a carpenter? -** He insisted on

having a dialogue.

- **It depends on whether you will be able to learn.** - I replied, getting up and walking away from the kitchen.
- **That won't do any good, you know.** - He told me while I could still hear very well what he was saying, and I knew what he was referring to, but I preferred silence as a way to avoid my own suffering.

Jesus was a very intelligent child, so I wondered what I could teach him. He had not grown up in our context and I did not know where to start, but I recognized the joy of having him back home. So, I decided to teach him the only thing he knew how to do well, that is, carpentry, and he learned quickly, starting to help me in small tasks, as my advanced age prevented me from presenting myself in the big projects that my children took on.

Quickly, however, my eldest son, who is also called Joseph, began to make use of Jesus in small tasks of family activity, such as cleaning, sanding wood or developing small furniture. And then he began to be known in our community, while I did not know if it was a good thing, because when his speeches were heard, the whole community would know who he is and from which house he came.

Time went by and while Jesus became an adult, I became even older. I lacked strength, my sight was fading, I no longer had the same disposition even to walk, much less to work. I dedicated myself more to prayer. I left the work in the hands of my sons under the direction of Joseph, who was the eldest. We lived well and had enough, but I kept crying out to God to change Jesus' destiny and not to let him drink from that cup.

- **Father, are you coming?** - Jesus asked, interrupting my prayer.

- **Yes, Jesus. Tell your mother to serve dinner and I'll just wash up.** - I replied.

- **Right, Father.** - Jesus told me.

- **Jesus, wait.** - I called him back as I washed.

- **No, Father.** - Jesus said.

- **Do you remember Mara's well?** - I asked.

- **Yes, I remember.** - He answered me.

- **What does that water taste like when put into the chalice?** - I continued asking.

- **Bitter, terrible to drink.** - Jesus answered.

- **When you talk to God, remember those waters.** - I told him, without adding anything else, and we went inside to have dinner.

Jesus' future was something I could not imagine, nor would I want to predict. As I watch him grow up, I feel sorry for the enormous weight that I allowed to be placed on his shoulders, and of which I was complicit and negligent. In truth, I no longer had any conviction in my own choices. What I did know - and hoped - was that the birth of Jesus had not been a series of sad coincidences, for a life is too important to be found amidst chance. All the other women raped that traumatic night did not find themselves pregnant, only Mary, and that could not be a fortuitous case, even if our miracle was only ours, for only those who need one understand a miracle, while those who do not agonize in suffering do not know the relief of a cure, those who are not dying do not know the pleasure of being alive.

Since the staff I presented never deflowered that everything was very confusing. I have always believed in the Bible prophecies and know that the heir to the throne of David was to return. I cannot believe that I was there accidentally, myself, a descendant of David. Perhaps my heart, which had already learned to be a father, could still be useful, and I learned to love him from the first time our hands touched, from when I pressed him to my breast and he could, for the first time, see a heart different from his own or his mother's.

- **Jesus, today you say the prayer of thanksgiving.** - I told him before we ate.

- **Father, blessed are you, Adonai our God, king of the universe, who brings forth bread from the earth; Father, blessed are you, Adonai our God, king of the universe, who creates various kinds of food; Father, blessed are you, Adonai our God, king of the universe, who creates the fruit of the vine.** - Jesus prayed.

- **Jesus, why did you add the word 'father' to our prayers?** - I asked.

- **Because if I think of God, I imagine your face, Father.** - He answered me, leaving me with no reaction.

- **What do you mean, Jesus? That is heresy. God is spirit, we cannot make an image or a representation of him.** - I questioned.

- **I know, but God is none other than a father, the father of us all, and there can be no closer relationship than that of father and son. Why can't I carry our friendship in my devotion to God? When I look around, I see us so different from each other. And yet, are we not the work of the same God? Yet some of us seek peace, others war, yet doesn't God love us both? Father, I know that I am not the one you wanted, I am not the fruit you expected, you stop when you are about to show me affection, but have you loved me less because of this? No, and it is of this love that I would like the world to be contaminated.** - He answered me.

- **Jesus, I don't hold back in showing you affection because you are not the son I wanted, but because you have a very hard road ahead, and I don't want what we feel for each other to serve as a block to you tomorrow in accomplishing God's purposes in your life.** - I replied.
- **Father, only this mutual affection will give me the strength to cross such a road. - He** answered me.
- **Jesus, I am old and I do not know how long I will still be by your side. A father's greatest fear is that of not being there to help his own son.** - I answered.
- **Father, if you share with me the person you are and not just what you know, you will remain by my side forever, for wherever I go I will take you with me. -** Jesus said to me, and I became speechless.

That dialogue had left me quite shaken. Before we went to bed, Jesus met me at the back of the house while I meditated on those words. Everything in me was changing, and I was old enough for change.

- **Were these ideas of associating fatherhood with God taught to you by the Magi?** - I asked.
- **Also, but whenever I was told about this divine return, I remembered you, and I have missed you a lot in the last three years.** - He answered me.

- **But when I visited you you hardly ever spoke to me, you were always with your mother and Gaspar.** - I replied.

- **Knowing that you were there gave me comfort, because on the other days I just tried to count the days so that these seven years would pass quickly.** - You answered me, leaving me in tears.

- **Jesus, forgive me if I have been absent, but the fate you have decided for yourself consumes me inside, and I cannot accept it.** - I replied in tears.

- **Things are as they have to be, Father, and we must believe that for everything there is a purpose. Did you know that I was born on the holy day of Zoroastrianism, before spring began, the last Tuesday, that's why they took the gifts to give in the caravan?** - he said to me.

- **No, I didn't know that detail. But gifts don't only have this meaning in your life, particularly.** - I replied.

- **In any case, Father, a gift is always a gift, a way of making alliances, of making peace, no matter how useful they may be. And I am a gift for humanity.** - He answered me.

- **Jesus, you don't know, you are not God to take on such a responsibility.** - I spoke to him with my voice shaking.

- **Father, a prophecy comes true only when we believe it will come true, and what better way to believe in a**

prophecy than by becoming a part of it? - He answered.

- **Do you want everything the prophets said and the Magi decided to happen to you?** - I asked.
- **Father, I say only that one day someone must bring that prophecy to life.** - He said to me.
- **However, it doesn't have to be today and it shouldn't be you. -** I told him, clutching myself hugged to his neck, and he clung to my waist.

That embrace lasted long enough that we didn't feel the hours passing. His words were tender and true, and they pierced my soul. I should not only teach him how to live, but show him how to live, giving him the assurance that in any adversity, while I was alive, I would always make myself present. However, it was useless to seek to keep him from that purpose and those prophecies, and in his bar mitzvah everything became very clear.

- **Today these words have been fulfilled.** - Said Jesus finishing the reading from Isaiah 61:1.
- **What do you mean?** - Nicodemus asked.
- **But what does this mean, Joseph?** - Gamaliel asked me.
- **Calm down, Gamaliel, it must be just an interpretation in the will to say that good things will happen to us. -** I was trying to reassure.

Some in the crowd said he was my son, who lived in Galilee, and I did not know what to say or do. The elderly elders wanted to beat him up, and I anticipated this.

- **If anyone touches my son they will be a defendant in a suit for assault on the innocent and false accusation in the Roman court.** - I shouted, silencing the evil tongues.

There was very little I could do. The teachings of the Magi had gone into his marrow, and could no longer be ripped out of him, they were already part of who he was. I didn't know how to behave, as I neither wanted to be invasive, nor did I want to further damage his training. After his bar mitzvah he was already a man and should be responsible for his own choices, even if these could severely hurt me. For my part, I tried to be present at every moment of his life, much more so that I would be at his side, but I did not have much health to accompany him constantly.

One or two days a week I took him to Tiberias so that he could have fun with others of his age. Sometimes we fished together in the boat that belonged to my friend Zebedee, now used by his sons. Sometimes I would just watch him playing with his brothers Simon and John, his cousins Matthew, James and Thaddeus, sons of my brother Alphaeus, and the sons of Zebedee, Simeon, James and Andrew, while I remained sitting in the shade of any palm tree. At the end of the day, we would return to the house.

- **Mary? I think I saw Gaspar's son watching Jesus from afar today as he played on the sea of Galilee. - I** said to Mary when we returned from fishing, still entering the house.
- **Are you sure, Joseph?** - Mary asked.
- **I believe so. I am, however, sure that those Magi would be able to keep him here just to observe.** - I added.
- **Perhaps you have seen wrongly, Joseph. I saw that boy leave with the soldiers who accompanied him.** - answered Mary.
- **Yes, maybe it's just my tired eyesight. -** I replied, not wanting to prolong the conversation.

I did not pay much attention to trying to find out whether or not I was the son of Gaspar that day. I sought to spend my old age teaching Jesus how to be a man, for if he truly embraced the road that had been set before him, he would need integrity and discernment. The years leading up to Jesus' ministry were almost entirely in my company. I not only taught him to be a joiner, but to be someone capable of finishing what he started, to have a goal and reach it with determination, and to always tell the truth to his face, no matter how painful it would be. However, when I found myself alone, either because Jesus was playing with his brothers, relatives and friends, or because Jesus was working with Joseph and Simon, I found myself thinking of all that I had done with Mary, in search of redemption.

- **We need to redeem ourselves, Mary, and if Jesus is really the Christ, everything we have done would have a just reason.** - I told him.
- **Joseph, what do you say? You know we can't mention these things out loud.** - He answered me
- **Mary, I'm old, I don't know how much time I have, I want to die in peace. No secret lasts forever.** - I said back.
- **Joseph, nobody knows that on that day my sister Mary Cleoppa, who is my twin, climbed the hill in my place. How can I say that now?** - answered Mary.
- **And it doesn't matter anymore, Mary. It's been a long time. However, we know that you were hiding in Alpheus' house while I was running to demonstrate my innocence, and to get your sister out of that situation. -** I was trying to explain.

\- **Joseph, because we had no other option, and I had been the abandoned one, while Cleofa grew up in the protection of our home.** - He tried to justify himself.

\- **Mary, the important thing is to have a clear conscience. While Cleoppa went in your place to drink of the bitter water, you were crying out to our God, in the house of Alphaeus, with Susanna and Abigea. When your pregnancy became a mystery to all who saw that theatre, you went to the safety of Elizabeth's house.** - I tried to explain, but she interrupted me screaming.

\- **Why do you insist on mistreating me, Joseph? Why do you do that? It's not my fault. My parents made that cursed vow to donate to the temple the child resulting from that miraculous pregnancy, and when my mother found out she was pregnant with twins, after the birth she gave only one of us to the priestly care, that is, me, me, Joseph, me.** - She said to me, shouting and crying.

\- **I am not blaming you, Mary. I am trying to show you that you don't need to be afraid of anything else, because God, by preserving you and Jesus, has shown that he was with us. I, when I drank of the water, was innocent, but God, seeing our plan, could have also killed us, but here we are.** - I explained.

\- **And why me? Why did they abandon me? If they had never abandoned me, none of what happened to me**

would have happened. - She screamed at me between sobs and tears, punching my chest.

- **Mary, do you still feel bad for your parents? But if they hadn't abandoned you, how would we have found each other? Don't you realize that everything that happened to you has brought us here? Circumstances are not always what we expected, Mary, but they always bring us to the place where we are today. -** I answered, hugging her tightly.

In fact, it was as if everything had been planned. A pregnancy in Ana's old age that, instead of a miracle, generates two, two Marys are born, and only one is given to the care of the temple, just my Mary. God's plans are not always the perfect ways that we imagine. Most of the time His plans are born from the most atrocious and desperate circumstances that we have to face. And out of such despair, Jesus is born, a possible messiah, the fruit of an ancient prophecy, but I do not want another messiah, I want only the one I have taken as my son.

While Mary wept clinging to my breast, I felt ever more powerless. Elderly, without strength, I found no reaction within me and my efforts to dissuade the path that Jesus was taking were useless. It was already common, when we strolled along the Sea of Galilee, for me to see him teaching his concepts to his brothers, cousins and friends, rather than enjoying himself as at other times. Those eight children were growing up under an interpretation of the law quite different from the one we were used to. Jesus knew that there was no better way to form disciples than to begin to teach them while they were still small, as he himself had done.

- **It's not when we have the answers or the explanations to solve a problem that it becomes easier. Most of the time it doesn't matter how we face the problem, because it simply doesn't have an immediate solution, and we need to trust that in this life everything follows the same flow and goes in the same direction or divine purpose.** - Jesus said.
- **Maybe you're right.** - replied André.
- **I hope so, for I have trusted myself to these truths. I never saw your brother Andrew the Simeon again.** - Jesus said.
- **He took over our father's boats and trade.** - Answered James.
- **But I am counting on him for this initiative of ours to achieve its goals.** - Jesus said.
- **When the moment presents itself, Jesus, for sure Simeon will be present.** - André said.
- **Jesus, it's time to go home** - I shouted from afar, trying to get him out of that conversation.

- **I must go.** - Jesus said, turning away from his friends.
- **Did the Magi teach you these things and tell you to make disciples?** - I asked on the way back to the house.
- **They told me that it would be much easier to change people's consciences by starting as early as possible. -** Jesus answered.
- **And then you thought about indoctrinating your brothers, cousins and the sons of Zebedee. -** I replied.
- **Not initially. I tried to teach back in the day when I just returned from Shiraz, remember? But although they marvelled at my interpretation of the scriptures, they would not listen to me. Then, when we were coming to the sea of Galilee to fish, I started to have the idea of starting with a small group of twelve at most, to remember the patriarchs and the tribes of Israel, but they are still in nine. -** Jesus explained.
- **Nine? You mean with you there are nine, fair?** - I asked.
- **No, it's just that Gaspar's son is following us from a distance. -** Jesus answered, perplexing me.

I was sure I had seen him, and that meant that Gaspar's son had been spying on us for seventeen years. Surely he was there only to ensure that the Magi's plan would come to fruition. I was repulsed by this reality, because I have never believed that the divine plans need human vigilance, and I began to advise Jesus to give up everything he had been taught, the person they wanted him to be.

Here and there, when Mary listened to our conversations, she would reproach me for instilling such ideas in her, correcting me not to encourage him to give up, and I would confront her violently in my old age, with arguments that hurt both of us.

- **Look at what you are doing to your own child. It is yours rather than mine, who are you to decide what he should be or do? Life is a gift from God and each one must decide for himself how to live it. But you and those sorcerers have filled the boy's head with illusions, he is not now a man because he has never even met a woman, what kind of life is this in which one is prevented from living his own dreams?** - I shouted against Mary.

- **I know you love him, Joseph, and that if possible I would take his place on this road, however, the Magi, or myself as you say, have only presented one road to Jesus. The decision to walk this road is still entirely his. Please don't offend me anymore, this is not my form of redemption, it is a burden that since I was raped I have accepted, and just so you know, since you don't seem to pay attention to anything, Jesus fell in love with Magdalene.** - He answered me

- **For the widow? So many virgin girls from good families in Israel, and he falls in love with a widow? And who still lives far away, in Judea?** - I replied.

- **I have not fallen in love with her, I just know that she is the best for me, just as I am the best for her. You still live love in an illusionary way, which can occur either within a legalistic context, or within a moralistic context, when love is the decision to do good to the other, reciprocally. Look at yourselves! I don't see a day without an argument within this house, and is that love for you? What good have you done each other?** - interrupted Jesus, who was listening to us in secret.

- **So you don't love her for her beauty or her looks?** - I asked.

- **I love her completely, for who she is and for who she will be, because her beauty will not last forever, unlike you, who took my mother for being young and a virgin, because you live within a context where the law seems perfect, when it only reveals what is bad. Look at what happened to them. The virgin was raped and they both lied to the priests, circumventing the law as David and Bathsheba did, so that today they can no longer live in union, because the decision to love her regardless of the inevitable circumstances of this life was not there in the Lord. I love Magdalene for who she is and for all that life can cause us, just**

as you love my mother, regardless of what you think of her. - Jesus answered me.

- **I love your mother, indeed, and much more than you imagine and judge, and I advise you to moderate your language within this house and to respect the choices we have adopted, for it is they that have kept you alive.** - I replied.
- **Forgive me, Father.** - Jesus answered and went away.
- **You know I love you, right Mary?** - I asked her.
- **Yes, and you know that you are my life, don't you?** - Mary answered me.
- **Yes, I know. Forgive me for being so unyielding.** - I replied.

In the end, muted by the wisdom of Jesus, we all knew who he really was or should be. Judaism had never flanked itself with the paganism of other cultures, but at a certain point we understood that the messianic promise made in the past should be repeated as the Magi had explained to us, for they were all descended from the same adamic root. Finally, we understood that that prophecy was not only our property, and that a potential messianic candidate would be able to assimilate within himself the differences between knowing and fulfilling, just as happened to Mary, since wanting to be the mother of the messiah is completely different from finding one in one's own womb.

And so our roles were not to just grow him up, but to create for him a destiny, a goal, however painful it might be for us. I, however, could not silence myself and tried in every way to spare him that destiny. But in my advanced old age, the projects made for Jesus' life began to take shape, and his faithful childhood friends followed him when he began to preach publicly. When Jesus presented himself calling them, their hearts were already faithful to his teachings and they understood that it was time. I looked at Jesus with the immense dread of not being at his side when something happened to him. However, I did not know what step I should take.

- **Joseph, Jesus is under heavy attack in Tiberias because of the content of his messages.** - Alphaeus came to tell me, panting.
- **Let's go and meet him.** - I asked as I stood up.

I looked for strength in the staff he was using for support, and ran desperately to meet him. Arriving on the shores of the Sea of Galilee, I saw the crowd surrounding him, while he remained standing on a rock, announcing to them the new message, the good news as they called it. I got close enough so that he could see and hear me.

- **Jesus, that's enough. Let's go home.** - I told him, interrupting his speech.

- **In fact, I tell you that the greatest enemies we encounter are those in our own house, who want to silence our voice because they are phobic about change.** - Jesus said, after he saw me and sighed for a pause, looking into my eyes.

- **Jesus, don't force me to take him.** - I replied.

- **Listen well, for you must not fear Rome, Babylon, Persia, Egypt or anyone who can take your clothes or your life by force, but only he who, after taking your life, can still give you eternal torment.** - Jesus answered in a loud voice, still looking into my eyes.

- **But what storm could be worse than the sufferings of this life?** - cried Simeon from the crowd.

- **To die knowing that your loved ones will still be suffering and nothing can be done about it.** - Jesus answered, addressing the crowd.

- **But what suffering is worse than death?** - asked André, encouraging the masses.

- **That of remaining in deceit, of living an illusion, for only the truth can free our soul from the chains that have been imposed on us.** - Jesus answered.

- **Enough, Jesus. This is not your obligation, you must not live it alone, nor force yourself to such suffering.** - **I** was trying to dissuade him.

- **It is, therefore, that the words I announce today are not intended to give you peace, but war. To set one against the other, brother against brother, until the truth prevails, until a change happens to us all, from the inside out.** - Jesus said looking directly at the son of Gaspar.
- **Simon, hold him from behind while Alphaeus, John and I take him by the front with the ropes, and so we take him home, before his words incite hatred among the authorities.** - I planned with my other sons and my brother.

While Simon was taking his position, going around the crowd to reach Jesus on the other side, Gaspar's son, noticing the plot, ran up to Jesus and told him to get close to the crowd, which was already about 500 people. When I met up with Alphaeus at the place where we thought Jesus was, he was already surrounded by an impassable crowd.

- **Why are you still here and do you keep invading our lives? - he** said, grabbing Gaspar's son by the arm.
- **I am the elder brother of Jesus, and I am the one who serves. -** He answered me.
- **"Isk arioth, come. -** Jesus shouted, preventing Gaspar's son from arguing with me.

JUDAS

- **There is a condition worse than death. -** Jesus taught.
- **And what would that be?** - I asked with a sarcastic tone and a smile on my lips.
- **The one in which you stay alive to watch the one you love die**. - He answered me.

There were more than two thousand of us, but those words came straight to my heart. That damn sermon had me gripped in every single way. It was right, and I found myself lost between my mission and the words of Jesus. Since I left Persia to return that 7 year old Jesus to his parents, much had changed in him, and also in me. I followed him at a distance, like a beggar on the roads. Every week my father, Gaspar, sent me resources to survive, but it was better to remain an apparent beggar and not attract attention. The mission that had been entrusted to me still echoed in my thoughts and I agonised between the fraternal feeling that I felt for Jesus and the duty to humanity.

- **Judas, do you know what you should do? -** Dad asked me before I left with Jesus.
- **Yes, I must hand him over to his parents and always follow him, but without being noticed.** - I replied.

- **Exactly. Write down everything that is important about him, always be in the shadows, but if by any chance he needs help, my son, do not avoid helping him. You will be his older brother and, as such, you should look after him. -** said my father, Gaspar.

I was only 14 years old, twice Jesus' age, and I knew nothing but Shiraz. But it was not the journey that terrified me, but what this mission might demand of me. I would face the challenge with the courage of a man and the gaze of a child. Two servants would guard us during the journey, yet I still felt incredibly vulnerable. With the dread of someone facing the unknown for the first time, I prepared our belongings, organised our animals, and we set off in the direction of Nazareth, opening the way to a new world, leaving behind everything I had known until then. I hugged my mother, Fatima, telling her that I would not disappoint her, while she looked at me tenderly and told me that I was already her greatest source of pride, and with a wave of my hand I said goodbye to my father, not knowing if we would see each other again, not knowing if he would love me even if I failed in my mission.

Ever since they brought Jesus to learn our arts, we have strengthened our ties. I helped him in his chores, I taught him his first steps, to play, to smile, to fall and to get up. However, at the age of four he was much more skilful than any other child, it was as if everything we were taught he absorbed naturally.

- **Judas, where are we going?** - Jesus asked me, interrupting my thoughts.
- **To the house of your real parents, and from today call me only isk arioth.** - I replied.
- **Isk arioth!? As you wish, brother!** - exclaimed Jesus.
- **Do you remember your parents, Jesus?** - I asked.
- **Of course, although I remember my mother more who, from time to time, came to visit me, not always accompanied by my father, but always by my brothers and sisters. I remember that one day my cousins also came.** - He answered me.

The journey was long and along the way we rested in our tents and dreamed about what he would do, what dreams he wished to fulfil.

- **I don't have many dreams, I think I just want to fulfil the purpose for which I was born.** - Jesus told me.
- **That's it? Nothing else?** - I asked.
- **Maybe, marry a beautiful wife.** - He answered me.
- **It would be more important to marry a good wife.** - I retorted.
- **And isn't it the same thing?** - he asked me.
- **No. A beautiful wife is not always a good wife.** - I

explained.

- **Got it. Brother, do you think I am really the one Zarathustra spoke about? -** Jesus asked me.

- **Up to now everything has happened as he had predicted, so it has to be, it cannot be a coincidence, Jesus. You are the one who had brought peace to all peoples.** - I explained to him.

- **And you, brother, what do you plan for your future? -** he asked me.

- **I only hope to be a good brother to you, Jesus. - I** answered.

When we arrived in Nazareth, I gave Jesus to Mary, as promised.

- **Judas, don't forget that you are my older brother, I won't forget you.** - Jesus said grabbing me by the arm and hugging me before I left.

- **You should not call me Judas, I told you, but isk arioth. -** I replied, returning his embrace and kissing his cheek.

- **Isk arioth? What does it mean, Jesus?** - Mary asked him as I walked away.

- **It means in Persian 'he who serves', mother!** - Jesus answered.

I went to live in the house of dependence on the

property of the prophetess Anna, daughter of Phanuel, and in the following years I was always following the growth of Jesus and watching him as an older brother, something that his real brothers did not do, because so many times they mocked him, treating him with disdain for being the chosen one, similar to what had happened to Jacob's son. But Jesus always had his father's company, which was different from what happened to me, for it seemed that my father did not even hold me in esteem.

Weekly my mother visited me, bringing me the food I liked, spending a whole day with me, and returning to Shiraz in the evening. Once a month my father accompanied her, bringing the money for local expenses and scrounging goods. I was a young adult living in extreme loneliness. And so I thought of approaching Jesus, asking him to keep my presence in Palestine a secret. But I had to study the habits of his family to find a way to approach him without being noticed.

So I found in Jesus' closest friends an opportunity, for it was common for Jesus to go to Bethany, in Judea, to spend a few days with Eleazar, Martha and Mary, children of Jairus, Mary's cousin.

- **I see you have found your wife.** - I told him, approaching unnoticed among the bushes while he waited for Jairus' sons to bring a rope or the stone balls to throw.

- **Brother! What joy! What are you doing here?** - Jesus asked me, hugging me, surprised to see me.

- **Shh! Keep your voice down, I don't want to be seen by anyone. I never went back to Shiraz, it has been my job to watch you from afar and protect you.** - I explained.

- **And why did you never make yourself present? Why did you never come to visit me?** - he asked me.

- **Because my father would not allow me, and even now I have come to speak to you on my own account. Forgive me if I did not do so earlier, but I did not know how to disobey my father's orders, for they were given to him directly from Baltasar.** - I explained to him.

- **I understand, brother, don't worry, everything is fine. How are you? Where do you live? Do you need anything?** - Jesus was still asking me.

- **No, everything is fine. Our mother, Fatima, always comes to visit me on the third day of the week, and my father, Gaspar, accompanies her once a month.** - I answered.

- **Yes, but where have you been living?** - he insisted.

- **In dependence of the property of the late prophetess Ana, now managed by her children.** - I replied.

- **Since we came from Persia?** - He asked me.

- **Yes. But then, is that the one who is to become your future wife?** - I asked, referring to Mary.

- **And who knows? I'd like to. She came to visit me in Shiraz, remember?** - She asked me.
- **No, I don't remember seeing her.** - I replied.
- **Yes, it was there on one of my mother's visits. But Jairus promised it to a rich young man. - He** explained it to me.
- **They are coming and I don't want to be seen now, I have to go. Jesus, no one must know that we saw each other. I will always come to visit you here, at Jairus' house, where we can talk without being seen, understand?** - I told him.
- **That's right. Peace be upon you, brother.** - He told me.
- **And also with you, my little Isa.** - I replied, smiling, and took my leave of the vegetation.

From that day on we met at least twice a month in the region of Bethany, and I followed him in the formation of his ministry that, step by step, began to gather disciples, starting with some of his brothers, then his cousins, then the sons of Jairus and, of course, I also followed him.

- **All the captivities that Israel went through had their origin in the disobedience and strong spiritual apathy of our ancestors.** - Jesus said.
- **And you say that today we are going through a captivity?** - Eleazaro asked.

- What do you say? What is the difference between this captivity and the Babylonian one? In that period part of the people was taken into exile, while another part lived in the ruins of Jerusalem. The only difference is that Rome realized that it was useless to take people into slavery if it could force them to work by contributing taxes to the empire. But, in any case, this is not the point, because working under these ideas, as you have done, for example, Peter, who joined the zealots, is not going to change anything. - Jesus replied.

- And what should we do? What did Levi, your cousin, do, who became a tax collector, working with Rome and betraying his own people? - Peter asked.

- Matthew is in there to learn how the Roman organisation works, all planned, Peter, for you well know that each one of us is a revolutionary. However, none of this will be of any use if our objectives are not well determined. We must recognise that we cannot fight the empire, unless the feeling of revolt does not flourish in all the people of Israel. - Jesus answered.

- And how can we do that? - I asked.

- Showing that we are under a new captivity due to the spiritual poverty of our priests, who interpret the law for their own benefit and remain in collusion with Rome in order not to suffer political oppression. The

priests and the rulers of Israel sided with the Romans through political agreements only to avoid going through the misery that today afflicts everyone in Israel. It is from this hypocrisy that we must rid ourselves. - Jesus explained.

- **It is something impossible, Jesus. It would be to reform the whole faith of Israel.** - Thaddeus warned.

- **The truth is that from anywhere and through anyone it should one day start, and I hope we will be the ones to do it.** - He replied.

- **You know the consequences you will face if you attack the Sanhedrin openly, don't you?** - said his brother Simon.

- **Yes, and in fact I am prepared to give my life. And it is good that you understand that this is my choice. No one will take my life, but since today I have voluntarily decided to do so. I tell you this so that when the time comes, if it comes, none of you will intervene, but trust in my decision and in the God whom we serve.** - Jesus answered.

- **It is just as well that our father is no longer alive, for he would never have allowed or accepted to see such a sacrifice on his part.** - John commented, remembering Joseph's death, died after having tried to prevent Jesus' first public preaching. Although Joseph's death was due to natural causes, Jesus still felt guilty and could not hide his tearful eyes when he heard John's words.

Thus, Jesus' public ministry began with a series of discourses that interpreted the Mosaic law from the perspective of human suffering, initially in the region of Galilee, where he was already known and could draw a large crowd, spreading throughout Judea and Samaria, until he reached the gates of Jerusalem and all of Palestine. His messages were an entirely human reading of the faith. All that Mosaic spirituality was renounced in favour of an altruistic behaviour. Jesus not only listened to the complaints of the Israelites, but he pitied them, he gave them love and attention. Watching him, I realized that more than twenty years had passed and that child, who had left Shiraz with me, had become my master. He, however, had lost that affectionate look of when we left Shiraz, as if he knew something that I still did not know.

- **Where do we start? I believe we should go directly to Jerusalem.** - Said Eleazar when we were gathered together in the house of Alphaeus.
- **My friend, you, Martha and Mary can always accompany us, but neither you nor they can be my disciples.** - Jesus said.
- **Why? Because of what I just said?** - replied Eleazaro.
- **No, not at all my friend, but because we must give Israel a sign, and my disciples must be a total of**

twelve, and all men. - Jesus explained.

- **Yes, even if Martha and Mary cannot, I could, and we would be thirteen.** - Eleazar said.

- **What I fear is for his health, always very weak since he was a child. I don't want something to happen to him unexpectedly, because I will feel even more guilty. It's a weight I don't want to carry, enough as I feel for my father. I can offer my life in sacrifice, but not that of a beloved friend. Besides, we will always be together and the house Jairus left you will be used as a foothold when we are in Judea, just like Peter's house.** - Jesus explained.

- **But my children will be in charge of everything with you, right?** - asked Mary Cleoppa, Jesus' aunt.

- **What do you mean? We have been together since the beginning, there is no precedence here.** - said Bartholomew.

- **Whoever wants to be first will be last, and vice versa Cleofa. Here there is no hierarchy, we are all one family, and I am the first to serve my brothers.** - Jesus replied as he did the work of the servants and washed our feet.

- **Not all, for Peter, Andrew, James, Thomas, Bartholomew, Philip and Judas are not relatives**. - Simon said.

- **I grew up with Judas and he has always looked after me for all these years, ever since I was taken to Persia.**

Peter, James and Andrew were childhood friends, sons of a personal friend of my father. Thomas, Bartholomew and Philip worked with Joseph, my older brother, who took over our father's business. So we are part of one family, because we have known each other since we were children, and if we want to change something in Israel, we must begin by unmasking the cynicism of the overbearing ones, who are no better than the other Israelites, much less better than other men. We will not be like the Pharisaic caste that says there is the message of eternal life, however, does not help the sinner, but expels him and keeps him away from the temple and from the services. Now, how can the sinner redeem himself if he is not free to present his offerings or to make his prayers? Enough of such hypocrisy and if we do not keep this conscience among us, we will do nothing and it will all be in vain. - Jesus answered.

- **And what shall we do then? What shall we do?** - Thomas asked.

- **Each one will have a specific and well-defined role.** - Jesus answered.

Jesus distributed tasks in order to make the ministerial activity more dynamic. In this way, the sons of Zebedee were in charge of supplying the food needs with the fishing work they inherited from their father. Bartholomew, Thomas and Philip were responsible for inviting listeners and spreading the word about the ministry in the regions we visited. Jesus' brothers and cousins would talk to the people before the sermons began so that the message would be able to alleviate the suffering of those present. I was in charge of administering the donations made in cash for tax payments and our necessary expenses, while the women welcomed the needy and administered the food donations, which were divided between the house of Jairus and the house of Peter, so that we had support in Galilee and also in Judea. During Jesus' sermons, we mingled with the crowd to ask questions and ask for explanations from Jesus, motivating everyone to present their complaints and problems.

- **You should not hate those who hate you, otherwise this cycle of hatred will never end. I know that the priests consider you as cursed and sinners because of your illnesses and problems, but if you also start hating them, nothing will change, not even in you. Loving those who love us does not give us any kind of pride or honour.** - Jesus was saying, at the foot of Mount Meron, with the mountain on his back and the plain in front of him, to a crowd of over three thousand people who had followed us from Capernaum.

- How can this be? Whom must I love to be honoured? - Peter asked.

- To those who do you harm, for hatred that is repaid with hatred breeds death, but love cancels out any feeling of hatred. You are not cursed or sinners, but blessed. You show more faith than all the others in Israel, for you endure not only your own pains but also all calumnies and slanders, discriminations and maledictions, without ever allowing yourselves to be discouraged. And you should be proud, for you are the salt and light of this world, for which our Father in heaven has sent me in fulfillment of the scriptures, after all, because of you today Israel can see the very pride that sinks an entire nation in disgrace, that manifests itself in hatred and injustice, but I assure you that forgiveness is the greatest of offerings. - Jesus explained.

- Should we forgive them for everything they do to us? - shouted Simon from the crowd.

- The offerings we leave in the temple what do they mean if not a request for forgiveness? But if we must sacrifice an animal or make any donation of our crops to attain divine forgiveness, how much greater an offering is it not to sacrifice our vengeful desires for the sake of forgiving those who mistreat us? The sins we commit are always against our neighbours, for we cannot offend God for what we are. Therefore, didn't the prophet Samuel already say that to obey is better than to sacrifice? And how do our commandments begin? By orienting us to love God first of all, and consequently our neighbour, so that if we are capable of loving, we will be incapable of committing the subsequent sins listed in the law, since sin is the fruit of a lack of love. - Jesus explained.

- So what are we to do? Give alms and fast as the teachers of the law do? - asked Andrew.

- Yes, but not publicly, not with the interest in rewards. Good must be gratuitous just as evil is gratuitously practised in this world. Alms are not a motive for vanity, but a responsibility towards our brothers who suffer in misery. - Jesus explained.

- What about fasting? - asked John.

- Fasting is an underestimated practice that should not be presented in the form of a suffering, for fasting is leaving the exercise of some daily activity to remain in prayer with our Lord and Father, it is not suffering hunger, but a pleasure in spiritual communion that makes us feel no other need than that of strengthening intimacy with God. - Jesus explained.

- And in what ways can we pray to strengthen our communion with God? - Bartholomew asked.

- Prayer is not a repetitive monologue, based on this or that prophet, for so many have not prophesied in God's name, so much so that even today their prophecies remain inconclusive and forgotten. Much less is prayer the pursuit of personal needs, for the true treasure is where the heart is, not where this world makes us appear to find it. Prayer is not an imprecatory and vengeful attitude, but the manifestation of love and forgiveness, for if you think that God will listen to a vengeful prayer, you must be careful because he will certainly also listen to the imprecatory prayers you make against him. Prayer is a dialogue that is not always answered immediately, but that generates pleasure in waiting, nourishing faith and trust that he has heard us. - Jesus explained.

- So how should we pray? Teach us, please. - Bartholomew insisted, clearly broken.

- When you pray, you must express yourselves openly, not ashamed of what you say or who you are, for God sees and knows you. Be sincere, breaking the barrier of fear and distance, for God is none other than a loving father. And think of what you would like to say to your father, as if he were no longer here and you had a sick need to have said some last words to him, more or less like this Father, you who are where I can no longer see you, and all that remains is for me to accept, with respect, this distance between us and this will of yours that hurts me so much, I would like to thank you for all the times we have shared the bread, because you have never let me lack it, and

because whenever we have shared it there has existed between us a sign of reciprocal forgiveness, in the same way that, by not letting me lack it, there still exists today the manifestation of your providential love, forgiveness and love that we must perpetuate by transmitting it to our fellow men, constantly imploring you to give us the strength not to manifest any violence against our neighbour, falling into the likeness of those who hate us today, we beg you, deliver us from such evil, amen. - Jesus said, without holding back his tears, clearly referring to Joseph, his father.

The crowd, silent, was clearly moved by Jesus' words, and their numbers kept increasing, so that when they entered Bethsaida, they numbered more than five thousand people, who had already followed Jesus for two days, and were hungry.

- **Jesus, where shall we go now? -** Peter asked.
- **To Judea. -** Jesus answered.
- **Then you'd better sack these people, because they haven't eaten for two days and the number is always increasing.** - Peter said.
- **Why don't you give them something to eat?** - Jesus answered.
- **How? We don't have but a little bread and fish.** - Philip

replied.

- **Now what testimony do we give to this people if we send them home hungry, similar to what the priests do?** - Jesus said.
- **And what should we do?** - Peter asked.
- **Take the boat and go catch more fish with Philip and Andrew, while the rest of you go and collect all the bread this people have.** - Jesus said.
- **Impossible for us to catch fish for all these people, we already caught fish yesterday and the fishermen went again early today, we certainly won't find any fish.** - Pedro said.
- **Now, since you do not have faith, I am coming with you.** - Jesus said.
- **I'm coming too.** - I told them.

So we got into the boat and entered the Sea of Tiberias. When we let down the nets we found no fish, and after we had let down a few times, Peter began to get angry.

- **I said we wouldn't find fish. Now we have no food even for ourselves.** - Peter said angrily.
- **You are always nervous, Peter.** - Jesus said, smiling, for he could not get angry, whenever he saw Peter's nervousness he began to smile.
- **You laugh because you are not the one who is hungry**

and you still have to fish for all those people watching us in admiration. I want to see you laughing when we come back without fish, what an explanation you'll give them. - said Peter.

- **You are the fisherman, you must explain how a fisherman, from a family of fishermen, cannot find a fish in the sea. -** Said Jesus, as he ran his hand over the water on the left side of the boat, further irritating Peter.

- **Oh, is that so?** - shouted Pedro.

- **I believe the fish escape because of your shouting, Peter. Have you ever tried casting your nets from this side of the boat?** - Jesus asked, referring to the left side.

- **This side faces the shores of the sea, i.e. less deep, how could there be fish on this side? You don't know anything about fishing.** - shouted Peter.

- **What harm will it do to try this side?** - Jesus asked.

- **All right, let's try it your way.** - Answered Pedro.

Peter then cast the nets with Andrew, and when he tried to pull her back to the boat, he needed all our help because he had caught so many fish.

- **But it is a miracle! -** Peter exclaimed, taking Jesus in his arms.

- **Peter, as my parents used to say, a miracle is something entirely personal, only those who experience it know it.** - Jesus answered.

When we returned to the beach, the others had gathered enough bread for all, and the fish we had caught served to feed that crowd and were still left over for the next day, when an approximate number of two thousand people still remained with us, who were still eating that bread and fish in our company. That was an extraordinary miracle and for two days the bread and fish that we had caught seemed to multiply in the baskets.

On the way to Bethany, Peter, not understanding well the manifestation of forgiveness explained by Jesus, because he still had in his mind much of what the zealots taught, went to take counsel with Jesus.

- **Jesus, I wanted to ask you something about forgiveness. How is it possible? Do I have to love someone in order to forgive them as much as Lamech regretted killing Cain?** - Peter continued.

- **Peter, when we truly love someone, we love them even more when they are in difficulty, we do not even calculate how much we have forgiven them. Love does not judge, it accepts. Loving requires time and because of this we must learn to forgive, for it is forgiveness that teaches us to love. It is there, when we forgive, that we learn to understand the other, to accept him as he is and to love him no matter how many times he makes a mistake.** - Jesus explained.

- **That's impossible!** - retorted Peter.

- **No. It is difficult, but not impossible, but I never told you that it would be easy.** - Jesus answered.
- **Jesus, this man came to us asking us to help his son who is possessed by an unclean spirit and who lives hidden in this region, near Gadara. - He** told James.
- **Then let's go to him. Do you know where he was last seen?** - Jesus said.
- **Yes, I can take you to him.** - answered the father of the possessed man.

Arriving near Gadara, at the foot of the hills surrounding that region, we met the possessed one who lived among animals, near the cemeteries, and who resembled the practitioners of necromancy. When he saw us from afar, he set off in our direction, overcome with hatred and with a frightening ferocity.

- **Son, it's me, your father, stop.** - The father of the possessed man came forward, taking our place.
- **I command you to sit down. -** Jesus said, with his right hand raised, taking the old man's place and immediately making the demoniac fall down.
- **What do I have with you? I know who you are, son of Joseph. -** said the possessed man, his voice hoarse, in a sarcastic tone.
- **I know who I am, but the question here is who you think you are.** - Jesus answered.

\-   **We are already many, and we call ourselves legion, because we have several personalities.** - replied the possessed man.

\-   **And I now command that all confusion be removed from your mind and that you be only the son of your father. -** Jesus said with his right hand still raised, and immediately that young man came to his senses and called out to his father.

Those who saw such a manifestation of authority were impressed, while we, his disciples, remained astonished and felt unprepared for such a ministry.

\-   **Isa, but what happened now? Was he or was he not possessed by demons? - I** asked, still amazed.

\-   **Of course he was possessed! -** Nathanael retorted.

\-   **But, what are you saying Matthew? Possessed? He was just disturbed. -** Thomas said.

\-   **Some say that it was a possession, others that he was only disturbed, just as they say that I am a false prophet and a deceiver, and others are already calling me Christ, and I ask you: what matters is what was afflicting that young man or the fact that he is now healed or freed?** - Jesus said, silencing them all.

\-   **My beloved Jesus, my brother is very weak. -** Interrupted Mary, regarding Eleazar.

\-   **Take me to him. -** asked Jesus very worried.

As we approached, from afar we perceived Eleazar's groans and that the situation was clearly urgent. Jesus had an afflicted face, pale, because the affection for Eleazar was immense since childhood, since when he received him as a visitor in Persia.

- **His leprosy is getting worse because of the humidity of Galilee and the heat of the desert. He must go home to rest for three days, and during this period you must make him take this medicine, and change the bandages daily.** - Jesus said, dismissing Martha, Mary and Eleazar in the company of Bartholomew, Thomas and Philip.
- **But, Jesus, if he doesn't get better, the authorities will have him buried because of the accusation of sin in the face of such an illness.** - replied Martha.
- **You keep him at home and do not allow him to be buried until I come.** - Jesus warned.

But the fame of Jesus was spreading, and many, unable to attend the Sabbath service because they were discriminated against by the priests and teachers of the law, sought Jesus for relief, healing or consolation. The crowd following us in Galilee joined the one waiting for us at Ennon, formed by the spread of Thomas, Bartholomew and Philip, but Jesus was extremely concerned about

Eleazar, whom he lovingly called Lazarus, and was already two days late.

- **Master, they bury Eleazaro. He had a high fever, and was no longer responding to any therapy, he seemed dead.** - Bartholomew warned, panting.
- **I told you to wait for me. Let's go to where he was buried.** - Jesus asked him.

When we arrived there, we met the sisters Martha and Mary, together with Mary, the mother of Jesus, who were lamenting before the family tomb.

- **Son, if only you had arrived on time.** - Mary, the mother of Jesus, lamented.
- **Remove this accursed stone.** - Jesus said, sobbing with tears, visibly upset.
- **Beloved, it is four days since we buried him, we did not know what to do in his absence.** - Said Mary, Eleazaro's sister.
- **He is not dead.** - Jesus answered.
- **I know that one day we will meet again...** - said Marta.
- **You should just trust me, because if I told you not to bury him and wait three days and you allowed him to be buried on the second day, the medicine I gave you did not have time to act properly. You made a mistake, he is not dead. Remove that stone, please.** - Jesus answered, interrupting Martha.

As we removed the stone, Jesus fussed and walked from one side to the other, weeping.

- **Lazarus, my friend and brother, come out, I know you can still hear my voice.** - Jesus said in a loud voice.

Immediately, to everyone's amazement, Eleazaro came out of the tomb walking and in health. We took him immediately to his home and fed him, and it was as if nothing had happened, as if he had never fallen ill. We stayed there, in Bethany, to celebrate the repercussions of this miracle, which had already upset the priests in Jerusalem. The feast of tabernacles had just begun and, with the miracle of Eleazar, Jesus could no longer keep his ministry far from Jerusalem, and decided to go up to the holy city and be present, performing many miracles.

- **Your sins are forgiven, do not be afraid, healing will come in your life.** - Jesus announced this to the sick who crowded around the gates of Jerusalem.
- **Who are you to forgive sins?** - asked a Pharisee named Raban.
- **Why? Is it easier to cure illnesses? You do not do either one, nor the other. On the contrary, you use the words of Solomon in Ecclesiastes and Wisdom to justify the suffering of others by accusing them of sin, and so you do not approach them to heal or to relieve their souls of the burden they carry.**

Hypocrites. Foxes. - Jesus shouted at them.

- **Master, all I would like to do is see.** - He said, approaching Jesus, a man who was considered blind by everyone since birth and who had been abandoned by his parents when he was still very small.

After taking a good look into his eyes, Jesus took some herbs from his pocket, spat on these until they formed a kind of paste with the clay, according to Jewish tradition, and applied that paste to the eyes of the blind man.

- **Now go and wash in the well of the envoy.** - Jesus said to him.

After washing his eyes, the man returned completely cured of his blindness.

- **I can see, I can see!** - said the man, surprised and as if he had never seen before in his life.
- **And now, cousin? Who had sinned according to our tradition?** - Matthew asked him.
- **But he does these things with his medicinal spells, possessed by Satan.** - Nicodemus replied.
- **You continue to use Solomon's words to justify suffering, and the figure of evil to explain what you do not understand. Can evil do good? Well, an evil tree will always bear bad fruit, and a good tree will**

always bear good fruit, for it cannot be otherwise. Evil, which is only a necessary agent for the manifestation of good in this world, continues to serve as an accusation on their lips. What is fundamental here: that the blind can see or that my methods are pure for them? It is true that the sight restored to that man is more important, but your complaint is not about this cure, for you are concerned only for yourselves, without any compassion for the people who suffer. The point here is that you can no longer understand the law in the prejudiced way you interpret it, for the discriminated sinners are now healed, showing that their infirmities are not the fruit of their sins, nor of the sins of their fathers. They are only sicknesses. Hypocrites! - Jesus said.

- **So what must I do to be as enlightened as you are?** - Nicodemus asked, in a sarcastic tone.

- **In his case, only by being born again. Purifying himself in John's waters, and going through a process of metanoia**. - Jesus said to him, referring to baptism and making him escape among the crowd.

The miracles and the content of Jesus' messages were beginning to annoy the priests and teachers of the law who passed into the temple every day on the occasion of the feast, and witnessed the crowds seeking in Jesus the relief those spiritual leaders refused to give.

The testimony shared by those who received from Jesus relief for their pains, who began to speak of him as the Messiah, the promised one of Israel, incited the authorities to confront Jesus publicly.

- **We know very well who you are, son of Joseph. Your father died trying to prevent your twisted mind from starting to preach your blasphemies in Israel. Joseph, yes, was a great Jew. -** Said Raban, attacking Jesus.

- **Jewish? What does this word mean but the claim of a people to think that they are better than all the rest of the world? Now, aren't the other men and women also the work of our God? Are not the people you discriminate against, by chance, of the same race as Noah? Are they not all descendants of the Diluvians? Whom we have been trying to exterminate from this world since the time of Joshua just for a piece of land? Hypocrites. These peoples that you discriminate against are your cousins, and in the name of God, for more than four thousand years we have lived a family feud, blaming God for the tragedies and misfortunes that we ourselves have sought. The truth is that, in pursuit of a false spirituality, we sacrifice our humanity, losing empathy for others and compassion for the needy,**

and surely it is a behaviour that shows no sign of understanding the law, for was not Jonah a prophet in Israel? Yet to whom was he sent to announce the divine will? To the Ninevites, the Assyrian enemies of our fathers and forefathers. Repent! Because of you Israel suffers to this day; you neither attain eternal salvation nor allow those who honestly seek it to attain it. - Jesus shouted in front of them from the open sky at the gates of Jerusalem, while all the people were amazed at these words.

- **Who are you to tell us how to interpret the law?** - Caiaphas asked.

- **I am the son of a humble man who, however rich he was, never changed his life, never raised his voice, never saw him murmur, grumble or curse. And you? When was the last time you heard the voice of God? You cling to the law because our God has been silent in this land contaminated by your debauchery for more than four hundred years. John the Baptist, whom you respect as a prophet today, was first called a demoniac because he lived in the desert. I live among the people and so you have found another one to accuse of possession, when you cannot even free yourselves and are all slaves to greed and money. A den of vipers, and I warn you that you cannot serve two masters.** - Jesus rebuked them.

- **It is our tradition that these people, for whom you**

have compassion, are possessed. - said Gamaliel, who was listening to everything with impartiality.

- **They are sick. What you cannot explain is not necessarily a spiritual curse, it is only ignorance. Now, the same tradition that teaches that these people are cursed or possessed teaches us not to respect people, to be charitable, to help the destitute and even the foreigner, or is it not Ezekiel who tells us to save the one who is lost, making us responsible for his blood? Faith is not the manifestation of the supernatural, but of an unexpected gesture of strength, when we have the courage to contaminate our religious zeal in order to have mercy on our brothers and sisters who suffer pain and misery. Faith is the decision to go ahead even when the heart wants to give up. It is a father who loses his son and, not expecting his return, finds the courage to live with his absence. Faith is the courage to love, and above all to love those who have done us wrong, those who have not known how to love us, who have abandoned us, because it takes much more willpower to forgive than to take revenge. This is having faith, trusting that the trial is only a means for edification.** - Jesus answered, silencing everyone and making each one follow his own path.

- **But there is nothing supernatural about it.** - retorted Gamaliel.

- **A miracle goes beyond an extraordinary phenomenon, for a miracle is just something we cannot yet explain.** - Jesus taught.

- **How is that possible?** - asked Thomas.

- **We always look for a miracle outside man, for, in truth, what we desire is only a sign of God's existence. The greatest miracles, however, take place within man, and are yet invisible to the eye, but sensitive to the heart.** - Jesus explained.

- **What do you mean?** - Peter asked.

- **When any one of us embraces a decision that is contrary to the vengeful principles to which we are accustomed, this is a true miracle. When we forgive instead of attacking, when we reconcile instead of intriguing, in short, these gestures go against human nature itself, and can only be miracles, divine interventions that happen not outside man, but in his own heart. When this happens, we feel a vibration spreading through the air, a wave of sensitivity that breaks the destructive pattern to which we are accustomed. A request for forgiveness breaks any sword. A hug destroys any trauma.** - Jesus said.

Jesus' discourses were touching, as if he spoke the language of their hearts, understood their needs, and was always ready to help them completely. There was nothing left over from the donations and we all lived with humility, according to the advice of Jesus, not accumulating riches. I, who was responsible for the finances, had saved enough to buy a piece of land and, instead of keeping that much money, I secretly invested thirty pieces of silver in the property of a couple that followed us, Ananias and Sapphira, thinking that, if the ministry grew beyond our perspectives, we would have a place to meet in the future to support the needy. However, Jesus' confrontations with the wise and religious became more and more constant, threatening the peaceful freedom with which Jesus had begun to teach.

- **You have no right to reinterpret the law and the way our parents taught us to live it. -** shouted Boncortassitis.

- **The law does not belong to them, for it is the divine manifestation to men, and therefore it can be read, reread, interpreted and reinterpreted, by anyone who is interested in knowing God, for it is a good that has been given to us to be shared.** - Jesus explained.

- **The law was given to Moses and from him to the people of Israel. Why should we share it with other people? It is our revelation.** - Caiaphas said.

- **But what are you? Blind children? Can one blind man lead another? Have you no fear of God? You use the law and ancient interpretations to justify the** murderous intents in your hearts. Hypocrites. You do not use the old interpretations because you believe in them, but because it is useful for you to hide the unbelief and rebellion in your hearts. Look at the entrance to the temple of God, the house where, with prayers, we should meet Him. What is there? A great marketplace for those who do not take the time to separate and choose the best of what they do for God, so they can buy at the last minute. Hypocrites, mercenaries. Damned. If you do not believe in these things, why don't you look for another activity? Why don't you go and work in other trades? I'll tell you why: because it is convenient for you to go to the temple and say that you are saved by being descendants of Abraham, when you are rotten inside. Hypocrites. The law is not a mechanism for their own salvation, but to announce salvation to those who do not know the law. Serpents.** - Shouted Jesus, extremely nervous.

- **The law is useful to us individually, not collectively. -** Gamaliel was trying to explain.

- **The law is a teaching principle so that the people may walk in the light. Moses, for example, sat from morning till night to teach the people the contents of this law. Now, if you, who presently occupy Moses' place, cannot lead a lost person to the right path, what is this law that you teach, what justice are we**

talking about? None. It is impossible that you use the law not to help a sick person on the Sabbath, but do not use this same pseudo-moralism when one of your sheep is lost or attacked on the Sabbath. A person cannot be less important than a sheep. And if you avoid charity justifying such indifference on the fact that more and more people will come to you, now the charity you do is not charity but vanity. You help the needy through a masked falsehood, when in truth you had no interest in helping anyone, because you want the favours of God only for yourselves, when the blessing that God gave to our father Abraham began in him to reach the whole world, all nations. - He attacked Jesus.

Hatred was building up in Caiaphas' heart for being shamed in public, and the voices that they were planning to kill Jesus were spreading.

The leaders of the Sanhedrin were looking for any reason to arrest and condemn Jesus, and they found an avenue in the person he loved most. The closest to Jesus was Mary, sister of Eleazar and Martha, who had washed him with ointment, commonly called a sinner because of her close relationship with Jesus, and because of an unconsummated marriage from which she had inherited the property of the promised bridegroom, a very zealous rich young man who had died of unknown cause and was from Tarichea, which in Aramaic means Magdala. Because of this, Mary was also commonly called Magdalene or Magdalene.

- **Master, they are already talking about your relationship with the widow.** - Bartholomew warned.
- **We need to organise the wedding ceremony.** - Jesus said.

In the days that followed we organised the wedding event, and the feast began while it was still tabernacles. When the representatives of the Sanhedrin heard that we were all in the upper room celebrating, they came to meet Jesus in fury.

- **Jesus, a crowd is approaching, ready to stone you with the Magdalene. -** Said Simon, the brother of Jesus.
- **Let them come in.** - Jesus answered him.

As the crowd entered and moved furiously towards Magdalene, Jesus slowly lowered himself onto the sand, and wrote.

- **There, they are over there. -** Shouted someone from the same crowd that days before had eaten from the bread and fish we distributed.
- **You are accused of prostitution and the sentence is**

stoning according to the law of Moses. - shouted Mordogin.

- **For what violation of the law? -** Jesus asked, still bent down on the sand.

- **Mary of Bethany was promised in marriage, Leviticus 20:10, Deuteronomy 22:23, take your pick. -** Mordogin continued.

- **And her betrothed husband died before consummating the nuptials. Now if the husband dies, the wife is free.** - Jesus answered.

- **This, according to tradition, should be given to the brother of her deceased husband, because even though the marriage was not consummated, she received the inheritance with which she supports her ministry. -** Caiaphas, who had come forward to observe the problem, retorted.

- **Tradition between families is not found in the law of Moses, it is only a matter of family agreements. Therefore, no law was violated. The property that this woman inherited was given to her freely by her family as part of the marriage settlement, and it was not her fault if the groom came to pass away.** - Jesus said as he wrote in the sand.

- **But your friendship is very close. -** Caiphas mocked.

- **Your father is my mother's cousin, we are lifelong friends, and what can you say against it? There is still a blood tie between us.** - replied Jesus.

- **But what does he write? Why doesn't he speak to us through his eyes?** - Caiaphas asked, not knowing how to answer Jesus, while the crowd slowly left.
- **Because you are interrupting my marriage with false pretences.** - Jesus said, standing up and allowing everyone to see on the sand the words "what God has joined together, let no man put asunder", written with the pieces of broken glass from the cups.

From that day they ceased to trouble Jesus, for they had nothing to accuse him of. When the festivities were over, we returned to Bethany, and while I was in the kitchen of Magdalene's house, one of my father's servants was watching me in the darkness of the desert, hidden behind a palm tree. In fact, when I went out to meet him, I was not startled to see my own father waiting for me. I knew that our reunion was inevitable.

- **Judas, my son, how are you?** - said my father.
- **Yes,**" I replied dryly.
- **I have come because it is time to take any initiative in this regard, Jesus' ministry is very big and there is no more opportune moment. Jesus must die.** - Gaspar said to me.
- **What do you mean by that? Am I now supposed to kill him? You told me that I should be his elder brother, and now I should be responsible for his blood? For the**

blood of my own brother? - I asked indignantly.

- **He's not your brother, Judas. He's just your responsibility.** - Gaspar told me.

- **And what do I do? I am not capable of killing him.** - I replied.

- **I have been here for two days only Judas, secretly observing your meetings, and in two days I have realized that the Sanhedrin hates you, because you are publicly shaming the teachings transmitted by Pharisees, publicans and Sadducees, and they can no longer stand you. Since you are not able to kill him, you can provide the environment for others to do so, even because his death must be a public event.** - replied Gaspar.

- **I still can't do it. He is right in everything he says and has a compassion I have never seen in any other human being.** - I replied.

- **I know. However, he will never be king or accepted in the Sanhedrin as a religious leader. He grew up among the people and not within the religious hypocrisy of Israel. Do you know that they have been plotting to kill him since his healing of Lazarus?** - Gaspar asked.

- **Yes,** - I answered.

- **So, it is something that we cannot avoid, but if it happens in the wrong way or at the wrong time, all the work of Jesus will be in vain.** - Gaspar said.

- **I'm still incapable. Do it yourself if you want him to**

die. - I replied.

- **Now, Judas, if that's the case, I'm going to cut off the financial aid I send you every month.** - Gaspar coldly attacked me.

- **But I live in rent here, I live in the service house on Ana's land. How can I eat and pay my expenses? - I** asked anxiously, especially because I had planned to replace the money invested in the land with financial help from my parents.

- **This is no longer my problem. You had a mission that you are renouncing.** - Gaspar replied as he disappeared into the dark of the desert.

I returned to Magdalene's house pale, lost and not knowing how to solve my problems. I knew I was, however, incapable of betraying Isa.

But Jesus already knew that the authorities were persecuting him, so he no longer gave his sermons apart from the crowd, but in the midst of it, to blend in with the people. As we reached the territory of Samaria, my father's words repeated themselves in my head and I noticed in Jesus a suspicious way of looking at me. It was as if I could not hide what my father had told me, in fact, almost nothing was hidden from his eyes.

- **I approached you initially for family reasons, but you did not accept me, I accepted you as my disciples.** -

Jesus said.

- **And by that, what do you want to tell us?** - Peter asked.

- **That one of you shall betray me as it is prophesied, and because it was prophesied, it is all as it should be. -** Jesus answered, and those words made me dumb, they petrified and destroyed me.

- **Why? I hope it's not me. Should I do it? I mean, should one of us decide to be the one to betray you so that the prophecies are fulfilled?** - Peter asked.

- **The one who is to betray me already knows what is to be done and knows that he is my accuser. -** Said Jesus, using the term devil to mean accuser, as he turned to Peter.

- **Peter, do you like me?** - Jesus asked.

- **Of course, that's why I tell you I will never be the one to give you up or betray you. -** he replied.

- **Peter, do you feel like my brother?** - Jesus insisted.

- **Of course, I already answered yes. Why?** - retorted Peter.

- **Do you love me? In the way that I have loved you, to the point of choosing to die in your place?** - Jesus defined it.

- **Jesus, you know that I love you like a brother. -** Peter replied, tears streaming down his face, as he threw himself on the ground hugging Jesus' legs.

- **And it is therefore that I tell you that unfortunately in a certain way you will betray me, denying the faith with which today I sacrifice myself for everyone,**

because you are not yet ready. You will not hand me over to the authorities, I do not think you are strong enough to understand that we must finish what we have begun. But surely one day you will continue what we began as a game on the banks of Tiberias. - Jesus said to him, referring to the ministry he had started when they were still children, while bending down to wipe his tears and hugging him.

I, however, left there aware of who I was. To make my situation worse, the money I had used was becoming necessary and, without the financial support of my parents, I could no longer cover our expenses. Lost, not knowing how to confess to Jesus what I had done, I went to the temple to ask for help.

- **Good afternoon! I wanted to know if from the donations and taxes left at the temple there was a possibility of helping an afflicted person?** - I asked Raban.
- **It is better that you ask any other member of the Sanhedrin. -** replied Abiathar.
- **Good afternoon, could anyone give me any information?** - I asked a little shy.
- **What can I do for you? -** replied Mordogin.
- **I have a job and my parents are rich, but I am not able to provide for myself here in Israel and I would like to**

know if you provide any financial help from the donations you receive? - I asked.

- **Are you one of the disciples of the Nazarene, righteous man? -** asked Caiaphas, who was approaching.
- **Yes,** - I answered.
- **I thought the support of Magdalene, Susana and Joana was enough. How much do you need?** - Caiaphas asked, ironically.
- **Thirty pieces of silver.** - I replied.
- **Just a moment. -** answered Caiphas.

Everyone withdrew for a moment and, inside the meeting room, they were talking among themselves. After half an hour, they returned with a bag and the silver coins.

- **We have decided to help them in this mission that they are developing.** - Spoke Mordogin returning from the meeting room.
- **But it is a loan, and in the future we will need it to be repaid in some way. -** said Caiaphas.
- **Of course, I understand and I thank you for the help you have given us. -** I replied, leaving.
- **You know it is far better that one should die for the people, than that all the people should die, don't you?** - said Gamaliel.
- **What I know is that one brother is incapable of accepting the death of the other. -** I told him, in a

warning tone and in a decisive manner.

On the way back I had that feeling that I had got involved in something that was impossible to solve. The days passed quickly and we were approaching the Passover. Jesus' ministry was growing exponentially, crowds were following him all over Judea, Samaria and Galilee, but it was still very difficult to get support in Jerusalem because of the voices that accused him of false prophetism and magic.

Because of this strange sensation, on the return road I had made up my mind not to touch those silver coins, using the few resources I had left.

- **Judas, early on I was looking for you. Where were you?** - Filipe asked me.
- **Sorting out some personal stuff, why? Did something happen?** - I asked.
- **It is that you should do the shopping, we lack fruit and wine.** - Philip replied.
- **Right, I'll get organised now and go to the market.** - I replied.

I had little money, enough for a few days, but I trusted and hoped that some donation or help would be given to us. The situation was very delicate and the contradictory opinion around Jesus had made him be received with honours at the Palm Festival, but the crowd that had welcomed him as messiah, was beginning to be influenced by the slanders of the religious leaders, and this was visible in the incoming donations, which decreased considerably. I had to do the shopping for the traditional Passover meal, and I hoped to buy enough for everyone in the cenacle.

- **Magdalene, I brought the shopping.** - I told her.
- **So little, Judas? What happened?** - he asked me.
- **I bought what I could with the money I had, and I prefer my name in the Hebrew form rather than the Greek.** - I replied, leaving to avoid further discussion.
- **Calm down, Judas. It's just that this food is for tomorrow's Passover meal, and so I think it would be more prudent to make it among ourselves alone, without guests.** - Mary, the mother of Jesus, told me.
- **Mother, I bought what I could. Perhaps it is even more prudent to begin to hold feasts among ourselves, for the calumnies of the members of the Sanhedrin have already spread among the people, and we no longer receive the same donations we used to receive.** - I tried to explain to the mother of Jesus.
- **So, Magdalene, we will do what we can with what we have.** - Mary said.

The next day, before the Passover meal, outside, at the entrance to the cenacle, Jesus spoke to those present.

- **You should not be surprised if because of me you are also persecuted. The hatred you have against me today will turn against you who have been loyal to me. But all hatred is the result of fear. Therefore be merciful. -** Jesus explained it to us.

- **We are ready, my beloved master. -** replied John, his brother.

- **Truly and truly, you are not ready, for you have not yet received the Comforter. -** Jesus said.

- **The Consoler?** - Thomas asked.

- **The Spirit of Truth, which is the message I have been announcing, that is, love for one's neighbour. When your hearts are free from all rancour, sorrow or hatred, you will perceive yourselves as brothers to each other, and true love sacrifices itself for the good of its brother. This Spirit will make you one, one body, for one purpose, and when this happens, you will be steadfast, for even if your life is taken from you, it will be taken for a greater good, for reasons that go beyond money, greed and avarice. -** Jesus was saying as we entered to celebrate Easter.

- **It is what we most want, however, people are extremely difficult and suffering has transformed them**

considerably. - Simon explained.

- **Suffering transforms us all, Simon, but it must never serve as a justification for us to do evil to our fellow men. You must keep your hearts in peace, no matter what happens to me, and never feed the desire for revenge, because I am only preparing the road, opening the horizons so that we can all be reconciled with our true and only Father, our Lord and God. -** Jesus said.

- **But why do you say these words? Must it really be so?** - Peter asked.

- **You must not let doubt haunt your heart, Peter, for it is an instrument of Satan against faith. -** Jesus warned by using the expression Satan to designate all and every feeling of enmity or opposition to unselfish good, to love for one's neighbour.

- **Show us this way then, Jesus.** - Philip asked.

- **Philip, I have been this way, this truth, the path of eternal life, for it is in love that we resolve all our conflicts and find God, for he is like a father who has four children, and each of these children evidently has a different temperament from the other, but this father loves all four of his children equally, so that he is incapable of acting harshly against any of them, always delaying his justice so that his children may have the opportunity to find the right path to follow. Now, when we perceive ourselves as children of the**

same father, brothers among ourselves, our hearts are in the Father, and the Father is found in us, that is, in our way of sharing the love we have received from him. Remaining in this unity strengthens the purpose for which we live, and if you manage to be just one, this feeling will be transmitted to others through such an example. - Jesus said.

- **How can people follow our example if they live under a reality and a model so different from the one you have presented to us?** - Matthew asked.

- **The only dualism that exists is that of light and darkness, and of holy and profane, that is, the ambiguous and complementary existence of good and evil, which are not represented in entities, but in behaviours and actions that determine which of the two influences our character more. People today live under the dictates of the world, which justifies its own indifference and evil in the guise of good deeds. When you are one, in the sense of living the purpose for which I sacrifice today, you will always be the contrast to the presence of evil in this world, and the light shines in the darkness, it is impossible to hide. All will see and follow, for light not only shines in the darkness, it brings out the path to follow when all is pitch.** - Jesus explained as he himself wiped our feet, doing the duty we had assigned to Peter on this day.

- **My Lord, why do you do what I should do?** - Peter asks.

- **Because one cannot learn to love without first learning to serve, Pedro. Don't cry or worry, just remember how much I have loved you.** - Jesus said to Peter, as he wept compulsively.

That scene and those words moved me, and at the same time filled me with anger for what I had done, for the choice I should still embrace, for my father's words, for what the Pharisees had told me. I felt as if everyone was looking at me with suspicion. At the table, while we were having dinner, Magdalene, as always, started the discussion.

- **Jesus, have you noticed that the donations are practically evaporating, they are no longer sufficient as before?** - said Magdalene.
- **It could not be otherwise when one wastes ointment to wash feet, donates the food one receives, pays taxes, in short, what do you expect Magdalen?** - I intervened so as not to be held responsible for anything.
- **Judas, you should have cash on hand anyway. And according to you, the money you had barely bought the food for the Easter meal. -** retorted Marta.
- **You need to check it out, because this is a sign that someone is deceiving us. -** Jesus said, interrupting the discussion.
- **What? Are you accusing us of treason? Are you**

accusing me? - Peter asked.

- **Pedro, you always react emotionally. I am saying that someone is betraying us in our savings.** - Jesus answered.

- **And who?** - continued Peter.

- **It can only be he who dips his bread in the honey with me. -** Jesus answered, referring to me, who at the same moment was dipping the bread in the bowl of honey, because, after all, I was responsible for the finances of the ministry.

Tears began to stream down my face. I had no way to hide my sin and my guilt. I ran away as Jesus called me, wanting to tell me something more.

- **Judas, everything has its solution. Judas?** - Jesus shouted.

- **I don't want to hear any more, let me go.** - I ignored him, out of sheer pride.

On that fateful night I went to the Sanhedrin as if the body was being led there. In my mind I thought it was the best, in my heart I knew it was the worst, the body would not obey me because even I did not know exactly what to choose. I was hurt with Jesus for exposing me publicly, yet I didn't know how to get around it.

- **Judas, what are you doing here at this hour?** - Caiphas asked me.

- **I have come to participate in the festivity that you celebrate.** - I replied.
- **Come in, sit down with us. -** Caiphas spoke to me.

I hurriedly chose a place and sat down next to Gamaliel. The tears still escaped me, but I masked them by saying a few prayers.

- **What's troubling you, Judas?** - Gamaliel asked me.
- **Nothing, or at least there is nothing you can do.** - I replied.
- **For every problem there is a solution.** - retorted Gamaliel.
- **I don't know how to solve the problem of money. I didn't use the one I borrowed from you because we will always lack it anyway, including the one to pay you back.** - I explained.
- **There is a solution to that, Judas. -** Caiphas warned me.
- **And what would that be?** - I asked.
- **It is enough that you hand over the Nazarene to us, and we will forgive the debt. -** said Caiphas.
- **What is it? How dare you make such a request of me? -** I asked indignantly.
- **Judas, I told you last time that better the death of one, than the death of all. -** Gamaliel said.
- **Is death a better thing? Where is such a thing written?**

In your damned teachings? In their interpretations of the Mosaic law? - I asked.

- **Judas, it is better that anyone else be the devil than you.** - answered Caiaphas.

- **You want me to hand him over? Don't you know who he is? Didn't he live by chance teaching here, within these walls, and you rejected him?** - I replied.

- **Of course we know, but the guards do not know him and we cannot go to meet him.** - Caiaphas said to me.

- **And why should I? He took me in and found me when none of you hypocrites had even realised that I thought I was lost. I taught him to walk, I fed him, I watched him when my mother was busy. Are you mad?** - I shouted.

- **You must do so simply because we have covered your debts, just as you asked us to.** - Abiathar answered me ironically.

- **But can't you tell me this sincerely, yourselves, priests!? What is this? A joke? A test?** - I asked.

- **Judas, it's the perfect moment. The militias are ready and if Rome makes a mistake, we can claim our autonomy. At least we will live without their presence in our land. Look what they did to us in Samaria. There is no longer a single pure lineage there. The condemnation of an innocent person is an occasion for the people to revolt. Was not this the purpose of Jesus from the beginning?** - Gamaliel told me.

\- **No. Of course not. Jesus desires that we transform one another by self-sacrifice, not by revenge or blood. Gamaliel, do you really believe that this is what Caiaphas intends? What if Pilate doesn't take responsibility for his murder, letting the blame fall on the crowd. It is Passover, I don't think you are so innocent as to believe that story.** - I answered.

\- **What is Easter but an expiatory sacrifice, Judas? Who is the innocent one here: you or me?** - said Gamaliel.

\- **The matter is simple, you got into debt because you stole your own master to pay for property and who knows what else. We have covered your debt, so either you hand over the Nazarene to us, or we will go to him and tell him what you have done.** - said Caiaphas.

On hearing those words, I got up and left in torment, not even knowing what to think, no longer having any self-respect. I felt as if I were embraced by emptiness and I relived the feeling of that day sitting on the hills of Galilee, listening to that sermon. It happened to me what he had taught, that the word of salvation does not always stay where it is sown, and in order not to find myself guilty, I imagined plans that were unthinkable to me before.

On the way back to the cenacle I noticed that two

temple guards were following me. I didn't care anymore, I just wanted to get rid of that nightmare, to return to the peace that had enveloped me until a few days ago.

- **What do you want? -** I asked one of the guards, holding him by the arm after having hidden myself behind a wall just around the corner.
- **We have been ordered to follow you to arrest the Nazarene as soon as you find him.** - replied Malchus.
- **I will not hand him over.** - I replied.
- **In this case, the order is to take you in his place, because you have used the temple's money and not refunded it.** - He told me.

The situation was more dire than one might consider.

- **What will you do to him? -** I asked, thinking that I could hand him over and during the process of accusation, in which they would never find anything to accuse him of, I could explain myself before all the members of the Sanhedrin and the temple, and return the coins.
- **The order is only to arrest and question him, nothing more. You have my word on that.** - Malco told me.
- **That being so, and if I have your word that they will do you no harm, I will take you to him.** - I replied.

When we arrived, the cenacle was almost empty.

Only Mary, the mother of Jesus, Magdalene and Martha, accompanied by Joanna and Susanna, and Porfirea, Peter's wife, were organizing the place where we had eaten.

- **Where are all the others?** - I asked.
- **They accompanied Jesus to the Mount of Olives for a time of prayer.** - Porfirea replied.

Then we headed for the Mount of Olives, but it was deep into the night, so I told the guards that Jesus would be the one I would kiss, so they could recognize him when we got there. When we got to Gethsemane, we saw the torches and the other disciples who were sleeping because of the food and wine. A little further on, kneeling and mumbling some prayer, I saw Jesus crying out, and I approached him.

- **Isa, why are you crying? What's wrong?** - I said, hugging him and kissing his cheek.
- **Jesus, he came with two guards.** - Peter shouted.
- **Judas, with a kiss, the same way you gave me back to my mother, do you betray me today? I knew that you were stealing from us, because when the soldiers came to collect the taxes from Peter's house, I realized that you had not paid our quota, but I preferred silence believing that you would explain everything to me. But today you have gone much further.** - Jesus said to me.

- **Isa, forgive me. I was afraid to tell you the truth and what you would think of me.** - I replied in tears, kneeling at her feet.

- **Judas, I explained several times that I did not start this ministry to be some other who thinks he has the right to judge the world, but with the desire to save it**. - Jesus answered me.

- **Sir, I had already withdrawn thirty coins. I had no way to replace it, I hoped there would be new donations, but suddenly we had no more tickets.** - I explained ashamed.

- **And for thirty coins you sell me? Is that all I'm worth to you? Thirty coins?** - Jesus asked me.

- **Isa, I went to the temple for help, not to sell it. They told me I should give it back, and charged me to hand it over or they would come publicly to expose me. They will find nothing to accuse you of, Isa.** - I replied.

- **I would not abandon you for thirty, nor for three hundred, nor for any amount that would require me to abandon you, for to me you are priceless. This is the only pain I carry today, but it is all as it should be, and you should not blame yourself. Something had to happen for this moment to be opportune, or none of you would ever betray me.** - Jesus answered me as the guards handcuffed him.

- **Isa, I was thinking of replacing the coins with the help of my parents, but my father, Gaspar, had asked me...**

- I couldn't finish my sentence because Jesus interrupted me.

- **I know, Judas. The Magi have been present since my birth, I knew they would use any ruse or ask anyone to have the prophecy fulfilled. The only issue here is that I would rather one of them had betrayed me instead.** - He replied, completely destroying me.

Peter, seeing the situation, drew the sword that he had not used since he abandoned the zealots to join the cause of Jesus.

- **I told you it was better to fight with a sword**. - Said Pedro, striking Malco on the right ear.
- **Pedro, stop**. **I don't want another bloodbath. Who chooses violence, dies in violence. My hour has come, just as they prophesied about me.** - Jesus answered and anointed Malchus' ear with healing herbs, stopping the bleeding immediately.

While they were taking Jesus to the temple, we all watched in anger. The other disciples attacked me, while I could not find the strength to react.

John and Thaddeus hurried to tell the women, and I preferred to accompany them. Arriving at the cenacle, they quickly told what had happened.

- **Joana, you must go to Cuza so that he will do what he**

can to warn the authorities of the injustice being committed by the Sanhedrin. - Mary, the mother of Jesus, asked.

- **All right, I'll go right now.** - replied Joana.
- **You, the older brother, who took care of him as a child, how could you be capable of such madness? -** cried Magdalene, but I didn't know what to say or how to justify myself.
- **Magdalene, it's no use shouting. It's happening, let's go to meet him, he needs to see us there, at his side.** - said Mary.

While the women ran, accompanied by John and Thaddeus, to the Sanhedrin, I lost myself in my own feelings and became aware of what I had done. In the Sanhedrin they shouted and spat at Jesus and accused him of having proclaimed himself son of God because in his prayers he called God Father. But he remained silent, his clothes were torn at the chest and he had been slapped.

Everyone was organizing to bring him before Herod so that the governor could decide on him, since no one wanted to be responsible for his blood, since there was simply no legal charge that could even condemn him to prison. But the soldiers handcuffed his hands and feet, putting heavy chains on him, and beat him all the way. When I saw this, I went to Caiaphas.

- **Caiaphas, Malchus told me that no harm would come to Jesus, yet your guards keep punching and beating him, you liar. -** I shouted at Caiaphas.
- **What do you still want? Our commitment has been honoured. Leave this house. -** answered Caiaphas.
- **Compromise? Here's your damn silver coins. Now release him, our deal is off. -** I told you.
- **It is late now, my dear Persian, for it is no longer in our hands. It will be a Roman trial. -** he replied.
- **Roman? On what charge? -** I asked.
- **Mutiny? Insurrection? Rebellion? Pilate will decide. -** Answered Abiathar.
- **Judas, it must be so. It is God's will. -** Gamaliel told me.
- **Will of God? What God's will? Your blood is my fault, not God's. -** I answered, withdrawing.

I walked out leaving those damn coins there. After all, they would no longer be of any use. Peter, who had followed me, was being questioned by those present at the entrance to the Sanhedrin, vehemently denying that he was one of their disciples, and as I passed by I looked into his eyes in admiration, even he who, a few moments before, had attacked Malchus with his sword. Agitated, I was trying by every means to find a solution, or at least to approach Jesus, but it was impossible. I decided to go to the land I had bought to ask Mazda or Jehovah, or any other God who would listen to me, for a solution, a deliverance, a miracle.

- **Did you see what you did? And now what? Who will take care of our son? -** Magdalene asked me, holding me by the road when she just found me.
- **Son?** - I asked.
- **I am pregnant. -** she replied.
- **Magdalene, I will always be responsible for my brother's blood and also for my nephews.** - I replied.

The guilt was growing in my heart. I returned to the temple and picked up the silver coins I had thrown away. I set off in the direction of the land, trying to talk to Ananias and Sapphira so that they would give me back the coins I had paid them for the land and take possession of it.

- **Ananias, excuse the hour, but do you know what's going on? I need those coins with which I bought the land, you can have the property.** - I asked.
- **But, Judas, we used that money, we have nothing at home, what good would it do you?** - Ananias asked me.
- **I wanted to get together with the money I have and pay for the crimes that Jesus will be accused of, so that he will not be condemned.** - I replied.

153

- **Crimes? What crimes?** - Sapphire asked me.
- **The members of the Sanhedrin are handing him over to Pilate accusing him of proclaiming himself son of God and founder of a new kingdom. I must go, I have to find a solution.** - I explained.

I went to the land, knocking on neighbours' doors and asking if anyone wanted to buy it, in a last desperate move. However, the more I tried to solve the problem, the more time passed and the less I found a solution. It was already daylight and the voices all over Jerusalem confirmed that Pilate would judge him in the public square in the morning. Under a tree, in that land of blood, I sat in despair, crying out to God for any solution.

- **What a situation my son! -** said my father, Gaspar, who was approaching silently.
- **Dad? Did you know everything?** - I asked in distress.
- **I told him he should die. I warned him. It is impossible to stop Mazda's plans. -** He answered me.
- **Mazda's plans? It was me who betrayed him, not Mazda.** - I replied.
- **God always works through our lives, my son. In fact, I think Jesus explained that very well, or did he not say that we are to be each other's miracle?** - He answered.
- **You were following everything closely. But, you are**

right, we must be each other's miracle, and I will be my brother's miracle, unmasking the existence of the Magi and the plans you have devised since his birth. - I warned him.

- **Unfortunately, I cannot allow you to do that, my son. You have done your part very well and we cannot obstruct Mazda's plans because of the feelings we harbour. It will all come to an end today.** - Gaspar said, concluding the discussion.

MAGDALENE

- **I am here, and I will not leave your side.** - I would tell him, without even knowing what to do.

My dresses were already faded with blood, his blood, the very blood of the one who had saved me in every way one can be saved, while I could not even ease his pain. My eyes were already lost in his, there where everything is said without saying anything, and my hands trembled, my arms wavered. I didn't know where to touch him, a crazy desire to say everything, to take his place, to absorb his pain, but all we needed to say to each other was unpronounceable, but visible in our tearful glances. He is the greatest love of my life, and the only true one. Perhaps much more, yes, for he is all the love of my life. And it was enough for me to see the world through his eyes. I did not want to go anywhere, to know any city, any person... no history, no information, no possessions, no achievements, no anything else. It was enough that he remained by my side. Whether or not he was the embodiment of our faith, living by his side was as close to God as one could get.

- **Live and be completely happy and preserve, at any cost, the fruit of our moments together.** - Jesus told me, his voice soaked in pain and tears.

- **I don't want another life. I don't want to share what I am with anyone else, for all that I am is the result of your touch. Before you, I existed in so much loneliness, satisfied for a day without accusations. After you, I came to exist through your eyes, for only you saw in me what I myself was unable to find. What will my life be without your presence? What will I... -** I tried to speak somehow, drowning myself in tears, but I was always interrupted, looking for a place on his body to touch him, wiping his blood, kissing his wounds, but it was as if my life had been kidnapped from me, and I was powerless to take back what was mine,

- **If you do not live, all this sacrifice will be in vain. -** He told me with a way of speaking that made him more human than any of us.

I already lacked the strength and words to express how significant he was in my life. He has transformed me into every atom that I am, and there is nothing more divine than this, and if there is, I don't want to know it. The greatest miracle we can experience is not the impossible around us, but the impossible within us.

I remember each of our discussions, the problems that came our way, the jealousy of the disciples, the religious accusations, and I admired his strength, the courage with which he faced everything, and the always gentle way of speaking. I admired his strength, the courage with which he faced everything, and the gentleness with which he spoke. And I miss each of our problems, because sharing life with him was the strongest experience of being alive and only with him did I feel a person, I felt loved, since we were children.

- **One day you will be my wife.** - Jesus said to me while we were playing near my parents' house.

- **Jesus, your mother is my father's cousin and I am promised to Philip, the rich young man from Magdala, disciple of Gamaliel, we can't do anything about it.** - I answered, ashamed.

- **For God there are no impossibilities, Mary of Bethany.** - She answered me, meaning that she would never recognise me as Mary of Magdala.

- **It may be, and if it is indeed the will of our God, I will be ready to accept it. - I** answered, trying to overcome my shame, not knowing that my heart was already his.

For those who followed the development of Jesus' ministry, everything was magical. His words possessed authority and power, they invaded our soul in such a way as to free us from all doubt, but above all from the fears that haunted us in that period of uncertainty. With his speeches, our hope was renewed and our faith restored.

- **Faith must not serve so that our personal wishes may be fulfilled, but so that our Father may make us capable of helping our neighbour, giving us courage and abnegation.** - Jesus taught.
- **Now, in this way, it is very easy for God to continue being God.** - I replied.
- **Why, Mary?** - Jesus asked me.
- **Because things do not happen in our lives, the prophecies are not fulfilled, and we cannot lament, because faith must not serve for God to transform this picture of our suffering.** - I replied.
- **Mary, happy is he who suffers because he loves God.** - Jesus said.
- **Jesus, we are not suffering because we love God, but because foreigners have subjugated us within our own homeland.** - I replied.
- **Any form of injustice that one suffers is a gesture of submission and love for God that manifests the messianic spirit** - Jesus said.
- **What does that mean?** - I asked.
- **That Christ is a spirit of continuous love for life and of vengeance against gratuitous suffering, which**

always arises in the face of violent injustice. - He replied.

- **But, Jesus, what we want is a practical, visible solution that will free us from so much suffering.** - I said to him.

- **Mary, that is called death. In this world suffering is the only constant, so much so that I have never promised you any form of peaceful life, but that of lambs going to the sacrifice.** - Jesus answered.

- **Jesus, we cannot feed ourselves properly because we have to pay taxes to Rome, which is not our homeland; we suffer constant death threats because of repressions against the local militias; our leaders are placed and deposed by Rome; our marriages are arranged for financial interest; we suffer silent oppression; what more can we give?** - I asked.

- **Mary, just now, in what you told me, I counted seven demons: lewdness, envy, greed, selfishness, unbelief, fear and indifference.**

- **But, I spoke from the heart.** - I retorted.

- **And I did not say otherwise, indeed, I find his sincerity praiseworthy. However, faith is not lived for oneself, but as a witness to others. And what kind of witness are we giving when we think only of**

ourselves? Are we the only ones in Israel who are in need? To be oppressed? Not to be conformed to our leaders? To be threatened with death? To have our possessions taken away? Are our fathers the only ones who, worried about the judgement of Rome, seek arranged marriages with rich families in order to survive and pay their taxes? - he asked.

- **No,**" I replied demoralized.

- **So, Mary, as long as we are each looking at our own navel, nothing around us will change.** - Jesus concluded.

That conversation freed me entirely from my selfishness, and I began to love him more every day, with the burning desire to get rid of that promise of marriage with Philip, praying and clamoring every day that God would hear my heart and transform such a situation, allowing me to escape from that settled marriage and run straight into the arms of Jesus.

It is common to wonder about the meaning of life and what it really is to be alive, because when we ask ourselves about life, we always answer what it is to live or how we would like to live, without ever answering exactly what life is. It is therefore that we define it as a mystery, as a miracle, because although we know what death is, that is to say, the end of life, we still do not know how to define life itself. And when we realise this, our eyes no longer turn to philosophical questions, but to the memories that we do not want to lose. It is to the memories that we attach ourselves and it is from there that our desire to eternalise arises. Eternity is not a theological concept, because one life is already enough for us. To continue one's own existence indefinitely is something we cannot imagine. However, within a love story, eternity has form and meaning. The reason for existing is to belong to the other who loves us, and I wanted to be entirely the property of Jesus, at any cost, and that story of ours that began between two children on the shores of Galilee, I wanted to make eternal. Every thing, every detail and every imperfection I wanted to make eternal. The jealous arguments, the contradictions of concepts, the days without speaking to each other, the kisses of reconciliation.

When we learned, however, of Philip's impromptu death, we felt relieved and guilty at the same time. We no longer needed to hide our feelings, but we didn't think that the solution to our problems would be solved only with the death of a person we cherished.

- **We did not know what we were asking for as we prayed, for indeed, for the law you would be cleared**

only if you were a widow. - Jesus said to me, very downcast.

- **Jesus, we should not harbour such feelings now. You always said that God's will would be done, for it is sovereign. Neither you nor I are in a position to control events, let alone life or death. That which was in God's plan has happened.** - I answered.
- **I wonder if it would be like this if we hadn't fallen in love.** - replied Jesus.

Over time, that feeling of sadness disappeared and he became happier and more natural. Life at his side was incredible. A man completely detached from dreams or greed, who kept his heart firmly in doing good for other people, and sharing not only what he had, but also who he was.

In Jesus there was no selfishness or envy, his ideas were clear and simple, which made them easy to assimilate, even if they were unique and original. He did not know how to harm anyone, and when we were married, if we argued, he never went to sleep without our reconciliation. We were each other's, entirely and indisputably, and we loved each other with a love so capable of overcoming any adversity. I know life only from him and I don't have a single memory in which he is not present.

- **Joana, why haven't you explained to Claudia that Jesus is the chosen one? - I** asked her in distress.

- **Magdalene, I haven't seen Claudia since the beginning of Passover, and from what I heard, Cuza begged Pilate not to get involved in the Jewish opposition. -** Joanna replied.

- **Joana, I can't stand it any longer... I am losing the only man I ever loved, and I find myself unable to save him, just the person who saved me. -** I said, choking on my tears.

- **Magdalene... -** Joana was talking to me when I interrupted her.

- **Stop calling me Magdalene. I am Mary of Nazareth, of Nazareth. -** I spoke to her in tears.

Mary, my mother-in-law, Joana, Susana, Cleofa, Porfirea and I followed closely the ordeal of Jesus.

The agony of his suffering was irredeemable. The violence against him was as if the hatred of Rome, because of the internal conflicts between Syria and Palestine, fell on his shoulders. He was treated as any thief, even if no one even knew what he was accused of. The force of the lash soiled our faces and dresses with his blood. The whip with spurs tore away some of the flesh on his thighs and wounded his head. His physiognomy was already completely disfigured.

- **That's enough! -** shouted Mary, my mother-in-law, in despair.
- **Mary, calm down.** - said Susana.
- **That's enough! Why do you continue to mistreat him? What has he done?** - Mary asked.
- **Your beloved son is accused of wanting to take Palestine from Rome. -** said Longinus, ironically.
- **But when Jesus healed you, at Cornelius' request, you all worshipped him as the son of God. -** Porfirea, Peter's wife, answered, silencing Longinus, who hurried to Pilate and asked him to stop the floggings.

In such pauses, every so often, we could approach him to clean his wounds.

- **My dear, why don't you stop this madness? What are they accusing you of?** - I asked in distress.
- **I am fulfilling the prophecy, my beloved and a prophecy, in order to be fulfilled, needs to be lived, beyond just believing in it.** - He answered me.
- **But I can't bear to remain silent and contemplate all the injustice they are doing to you. -** I told him.
- **Mary, my Mary, only my body suffers. My soul is at peace. And my brother, Judas? Any news?** - he asked, worried.

- **Jesus, aren't you suffering too much already to still worry about who betrayed you?** - I rebutted the question, indignant.
- **Mary, and Judas?** - he insisted.
- **He's dead, Jesus. The cause is still uncertain, but it seems he committed suicide.** - I answered sighing.
- **My brother.** - Jesus said, crying.
- **Don't be like that, my love.** - I tried to console him.
- **Mary, it was not his fault, but this prophecy that needed to happen. And even less do I think he committed suicide. It goes against the teaching of the Magi. Surely he was silenced so that he would not be interrogated during my trial.** - He answered me, while he was dragged by the soldiers for another round of floggings.

None of us had ever seen such strength and determination. It was inexplicably divine.

We did not all know what had actually happened in Persia and what he had been taught and forced to be. We knew that Judas was the eldest son of Gaspar, and that although he was responsible for the prophecy being fulfilled in the life of Jesus, in time he had been converted and became more and more attached to the cause of his brother Isa, as he called him, without ever thinking that his death was really necessary. In fact, Jesus' death, however much he warned us about it, was always unimaginable for us. I believe that no one, however spiritual they may be, can absorb the idea of a necessary death for someone they love.

- **I don't understand your insistence on dying, Jesus. Didn't God provide the lamb for Abraham?**" asked Judas after some explanations from Jesus, meaning that any providence would also come upon his life.

- **Judas, the sacrifice I make is substitutionary, so that no other sacrifice is necessary. It is known that the remission of sins takes place only by shedding blood, and not sacrificing Isaac, who was a man and innocent, does not seem to have been a wise decision, for any animal sacrifice is incomplete. For human sin a just and righteous human sacrifice is required, nullifying the guilt of Adam's disobedience.** - Jesus explained.

Those words repeated themselves in my thoughts on the terrifying moment we were witnessing. None of us had ever imagined that such a monstrosity would one day come true. How could someone who had done only good to all be condemned? On what charge? Doing good? Our hope was that all that Rome would be used as an example against the real militants, but that the suffering of Jesus would end in that punishment, not going any further.

- **Here is Jesus of Nazareth, the son of Joseph, duly punished, and he will certainly not make the same mistakes again.** - Pilate was announcing to the crowd.
- **He is a rebel and this will not stop him.** - shouted Caiaphas.
- **And what else am I supposed to do? This man is innocent.** - said Pilate.
- **Pilate, don't get involved in this religious problem, it is not common Roman practice. It is passover, present another prisoner with Jesus and let them decide which of the two to release.** - Cuza advised.
- **Pilate, that is a holy man.** - Claudia, Pilate's wife, warned him about Jesus.

Pilate, turning to the crowd, had another prisoner brought in to let the people decide which of the two to condemn, in the hope that they would spare Jesus.

- **Well, here we have Jesus of Nazareth, against whom there is no accusation and therefore I publicly wash my hands of him. And, on the other side, we have Barabbas, the other Jesus who proclaims himself the saviour of the Jews. Since it is Passover, I offer forgiveness to one of the two. Which Jesus should I spare? Choose.** - Said Pilate, washing his hands as a sign of innocence for the decision of the people about the life of Jesus, and presenting the other prisoner, the leader of the Zealots, Barabbas, who called himself Jesus Barabbas, and claimed to be the liberator of Israel.

At first nobody said anything. There was complete silence, until someone in the crowd began to incite them to release Barabbas. We were all amazed at the masses that gradually acclaimed Barabbas as the hero of the people. We desperately tried to silence that mad shouting and to find the person who was encouraging the release of Barabbas, until we found Gaspar who was moving among the crowd, convincing the masses. However much we ran to silence him, those present had already decided on the condemnation of Jesus, so much so that we no longer knew what to do, and whether it had all been a prophecy or a terrible curse.

- **But what are you doing, you cursed man?** - Peter said furiously, taking Gaspar by the clothes as soon as he reached him.
- **My brothers and I are saving humanity and making Jesus an indelible memory in history, without publicly denying him as you did.** - He answered Peter, destroying his arguments and making me look around and see among the crowd other Magi, including Baltasar and Belchior.
- **Are you people crazy? Condemning an innocent to save the world?** - I questioned him.

- **Would it be better to save Jesus and condemn the world?** - He asked me.
- **Anyone but my husband.** - I replied.
- **You met him already knowing what you were destined for and yet you chose to marry him. What you are suffering today was your choice.** - answered Gaspar.
- **What we have suffered today, you wretch.** - said Peter, passing his sword through Gaspar's belly.
- **Peter, this can neither stop us nor kill me.** - Gaspar said, as he withdrew from the crowd and his body turned into light.
- **Pedro, what's going on?** - I asked.
- **I don't know, I don't know.** - Pedro said, as he ran away in terror.
- **Mary, we must go back to Jesus, forget the rest.** - Said Porfirea pulling me by the arm.

We ran towards Jesus in the hope of seeing him, while I had the need to embrace him, to take him for myself, to get him out of that chaotic situation. Pilate, through the intercession of Cuza and Claudia, allowed us a few minutes with Jesus, but there was the consternation of silence in our souls. Mary, Cleopha, Susanna, Joanna, Porfirea, John, Thaddeus, James, Martha and I looked at Jesus without being able to pronounce anything but the sadness that filled our gaze.

- **Why don't you defend yourself? -** questioned James, his cousin.

- **Have you ever seen such a trial? Where someone is openly accused of something they never committed and instead of the crowd shouting for their innocence, they shout for their conviction? Is this a coincidence for you? I am renewing all things. -** Jesus answered.

- **Gaspar was in the crowd seducing her against you. -** Said Mary, his mother.

- **Gaspar is not God, only his messenger. -** Jesus said, without our understanding what he was referring to.

- **But I don't want a messiah, I just want you, your son needs you. -** I told him.

- **You mean my children, for I know they are twins by the size of their bellies. I love you and I already love them with all that I am. -** he said to me.

- **Jesus, so we need you even more with us. -** I answered, crying and kissing him.

- **My beloved, this is a moment in which I need strength. Do you think that I have not thought of abandoning everything and coming back to you? I have thought many times, but I would show weakness, apostasy, an attitude from which I would be defeated and the world would remain the same. Everything will be different after this judgement and I will continue to be present with you. -** Jesus answered.

- **What do you mean? Are you going to resurrect?** - asked John.
- **John, death is only a stage of life.** - Jesus said.
- **But if you will still be there, then you will not have died.** - James said.
- **Resurrection is nothing but the will to not remain dead, and this will is found in my messages and in your hearts. Love is the only sentiment willing to go beyond life. Each time you announce my name and what I have taught, I will make myself present, resurrected in your midst through your thoughts and in your hearts. Each time you feed the hungry, give drink to the thirsty, clothe the naked, and visit those in prison, those who cannot and no longer have the strength to fight their own battles and fight for their lives, I will be present.** - Jesus explained.
- **But it is not enough for us. It will never be enough.** - Said Mary, his mother.
- **That will be more than enough, mother, for you will still have your children who love you, making your memories come alive.** - Jesus answered, referring to John and Simon and their sisters.
- **However, I will have no one.** - I have spoken.
- **How can you say that when you carry in your womb the fruit of our love? Love them and you will see me in them.** - Jesus replied, being dragged to the crucifixion by the guards.

- **No, no. Give me back my husband. No... I want my love, I am his and he is mine, father of my children, treasure of my heart, my everything, my reason, my whys... They are tearing everything I have away from me.** - I screamed uncontrollably, while Joana tried to calm me down.

When I regained my courage, I continued to follow him from afar, as far as I was allowed to stay, observing everything in tears. In prison, they mocked him, flogged him, spat on him, tore his clothes and dressed him in a piece of cloth reddened with his blood, placing a crown of thorns on his head.

- **The one claiming to be the saviour of Israel was the other Jesus you freed, Barabbas.** - I shouted from the courtyard.
- **We did not free Barabbas, but your people chose to crucify this Jesus. -** Said Cornelius, the centurion.
- **However, my husband never called himself king or saviour of Israel.** - I replied.
- **Why, then, does he not escape? He has worked so many miracles and he cannot solve this simple problem? Just plead his innocence and confirm that he said nothing of what he is accused of.** - Said Cornelius.

I didn't know what to answer. The people he defended so much were present when they decided for his crucifixion, and none of them, not even those healed or freed, came out in his defence.

- **Because loving is a gesture of surrender, not a demand. To love is the desire to save the lost, not to save oneself. Now, isn't that what soldiers do, that is, they go into battle for the good of those they love and the nation they defend? Are not soldiers the first to lay down their lives for the ideals they protect?** - Jesus answered from inside the prison, leaving Cornelius ashamed.

While his physiognomy was transformed by the harsh aggressions he suffered, his eyes remained transmitting the same unaltered peace. They handcuffed his feet to their waists, placed the cross on his shoulders, and the march outside the city walls began. Jesus could not drink water or have any pause for breath.

I tried hard to get them to let me pass to his aid, but they kept saying that as long as he could carry, no help would be allowed. Simon, who was absent because he had gone to ask Joseph, Jesus' older brother on his father's side, for help, looked on in astonishment.

- **But it is Easter... how is it possible that a trial could** have taken place so quickly? I arrived too late! -** exclaimed Simon, surprised.

- **Simon, it's not your fault. Did you come with Joseph? -** I asked.

- **Yes, it's a little further on. -** Simon replied.

Joseph, seeing that scene, tried to use his influence.

- **I am Joseph, son of Joseph the carpenter, we have orders all over Jerusalem, I can pay for the absolution of Jesus, my brother. -** Joseph said to Longinus.

- **It is impossible, because all the Jewish people chose to condemn him by freeing Barabbas. -** Longino replied.

- **All these people preferred Barabbas to my brother? Damned people, then they don't know why God doesn't answer their prayers. -** Said Joseph, as Jesus passed by, collapsing under the weight of the cross.

- **Are you family? Help him. -** Said Private Stephaton.

- **Just now. -** said Joseph, running to Jesus' aid. - **My brother, how can I help you?**

- **You are already doing it, Joseph. Looking at him reminds me so much of him,"** Jesus said, referring to Joseph, his father.

- **My brother, forgive me, I have always been so impatient and I always criticised you when you were younger. -** said Joseph.

- **It's OK, Joseph. It's in the past, the important thing is that we are here now and can still forgive each other.** - Jesus answered.
- **I have nothing to forgive you for, you're just a source of pride.** - replied Joseph.
- **Me? The illegitimate son? I have nothing to be proud of but the opportunity to have been a brother to all of you and to have been part of this beautiful family.** - Jesus said, tearing Joseph's tears.
- **Enough, he can continue alone now.** - Said Stephaton, seeing the closeness and dialogue of the two, returning the cross to Jesus and removing Joseph from his side.

The road was almost finished and we were approaching the hill called the skull, which was so called because of the corpses that accumulated in the mass grave behind the place where the condemned were crucified. When we arrived there, Jesus collapsed on the cross he was carrying and was awakened only by the soldiers positioning his body.

- **Have mercy, I beg you.** - I shouted as they placed the body of Jesus on the cross to drive the nails through.
- **Father, have mercy on them for they are only fulfilling your eternal purposes.** - Said Jesus, awakened by the terrible pain, as Longinus pierced his wrists and Stephaton his heels.

The scene was a spectacle for those watching and a tragedy for any family member. It was unbearable to contemplate. Those who continued to watch had in their eyes the desire for a miracle, the hope that something would happen, but when God decides to remain immobile, not even the wind blows to relieve the heat, nothing wipes away our tears, and the semblance of hope step by step gives way to despair, until we become aware that nothing will change.

- **My son... what have I done?** - said Mary, at the foot of the cross.

- **Everything was as it had to be and you should rejoice that you still have other children to embrace.** - Said Jesus, referring to his brothers and sisters.

- **And me? What will I hug tonight but an empty sheet?** - I told Jesus.

- **Freedom, my love, I die so that you may live fully and abundantly.** - Jesus answered.

Life? What life? That was a dialogue I wanted to avoid, because it was repeating itself as when it all began, terribly prophetic and true.

- **And when I am gone, life will never be the same again, for we will be reconciled with God.** - Jesus was explaining the purpose of his ministry to me one starry night on the shores of Lake Tiberias.

- **And what life will I have without you?** - I mumbled.
- **Your life will be like the sky for me, my beloved, which will always be empty while you are not there. But when you come to Tiberias, lie on the sand, near the sea, and look at the sky, as we are doing now, and we will meet here, under our sky of stars, you on the sand of the beach and me in the sky reflected in the sea, so that every time you dip your body in these waters, I will be embracing you.** - Jesus said to me, while gently bathing me in the sea.

While the memories invaded me, life abandoned him. Slowly his head rested on his chest, while he, almost unconscious, remembered his father Joseph, in the visible and intimate suffering he was going through.

- **Father, why have you abandoned me?** - Jesus shouted, and we did not know whether he was referring to God or to Joseph.
- **Your father is dead, my son, and it's just as well that he is, because he would never allow so much suffering to befall him.** - Said Mary, his mother.
- **It no longer matters, for it is all finished.** - Jesus replied, breathing out.

The guards had accelerated the process of killing the other condemned men, but, fearful of the healing he had received, Longinus avoided breaking Jesus' legs by piercing his right side with the point of a spear. He was already dead, but water and blood still gushed out distinctly, two elements of life coming out of the same wound. Everyone was terrified and some witnessed small tremors throughout Jerusalem, tearing the veil of the temple that separated the holy place from the most holy.

To witness, helplessly, the death of a loved one is the worst of all punishments. Jesus was right when he said that there are worse moments than death in this life, and my worst moment was receiving the lifeless body of my husband wrapped in linen cloths that we had bought. Mary, the mother of Jesus, and I asked the others to leave us alone for a few minutes, so we stooped down at the foot of that accursed cross and embraced his lifeless body.

Everything was very strange, just yesterday we celebrated Easter in his company and the next day he was our Paschal sacrifice. Embraced by his body, we remained in disbelief. The authorities wanted to take him from us claiming that he had been condemned as a criminal, but Joseph, his brother, paid for his body to be returned to us, using the gold that the Magi had donated at his birth.

- **Joseph, have you brought the rest of the presents so that we can clean his body?** - Mary asked.

- **Yes, they are already at the entrance to our family**

mausoleum. - answered Joseph.

- **What are you going to do now?** - insisted Mary.

- **I don't know, continuing with family activities. Everything is still very recent and I can't assimilate. I will return to Arimatea with my family. You remain attentive and vigilant, for the situation here is still very nervous.** - He warned Joseph that, to distinguish himself from his father, we called Joseph Arimatea, while he left with his wife and children.

I cleaned my husband's body, together with Mary, anointed his wounds, washed him with myrrh, wrapped him with linen cloths and let the incense burn, all the while kissing his body, his face, begging him to perform one last miracle and return home with me.

Grief teaches that in despair everything can still get worse, that there is never an end to suffering, that we only learn to live with that which ruins us from within and which every day robs us of the desire to get up, to open the window, to see the world. Widowhood is not accepting death, it is dealing with absence, with emptiness. It is a rite of getting up each day looking for hope and striving not only to keep alive the memory of the one who has gone, but to survive from those memories, because they serve much more to encourage us to live, than to continue the memory of the one who has left us.

For the funeral the others who were following us came to help, together with the disciples.

- **Do we know anything about Judas?** - Thomas asked.
- **Still nothing.** - replied Bartholomew.
- **Very strange.** - agreed James.
- **I think we should spread out for a while.** - Thaddeus said.
- **On the contrary, now that we must remain more united. We have the cenacle and it is best that we are together, looking after one another.** - Peter said.
- **For the time being we could not even think, and we returned to Nazareth. -** I told them, warning them that I would return home with my mother-in-law.
- **Yes, let's wait for the mourning to pass and we'll go back home.** - Mary agreed with me.

The time we spent in the cenacle was unbearable for me. I could not digest the acceptance visible on the faces of the others and therefore I could not be in the same environment with them. I could not bear to remember the teachings of Jesus, nor his words, because the absence of his touch hurt me. The image of his dead body in my arms was etched in my eyes, and I saw it wherever I looked and wherever I went. I was hardly ever inside the cenacle because everything there reminded me of Jesus. I couldn't wait for those three days to pass and I could return to

Nazareth, lock myself in a room and wait to die. Longing is something that we can define only when we realize that the presence of all the others is insufficient to fill the hole of the absence of the one who died.

After the three days, I went early in the morning to visit the tomb, to leave there my prayers, my supplications, my anguish? everything just a picture to be interpreted, because what I really hoped was that he would come out healed from that tomb as it had happened to Eleazar, or to go back running to Nazareth, finally, to get rid of such a longing. However, as I approached the place, I noticed a commotion that quickly dissipated.

On arriving before the tomb I saw the fallen stone, but the Roman seals intact, and that human figure in the form of a light, sitting on the removed stone. The same light that had emanated from Gaspar when Peter struck him with the sword.

- **You? Always you behind everything, all the time. After all, what do you want? What are you doing here? Why is the tomb open?** - I told you.

- **Yes, always I. In all that is alive, I am, and what I do now, none of you can yet understand. His sacrifice has been accepted and here is no longer his place. -** That light answered me.

- **What do you mean by that? Is he alive?** - I asked.

- **What are you doing here? What are you looking for? He is no longer among the living and at the same time he remains alive, inside you.** - He answered me pointing to my belly, referring to our children.
- **Who are you? Gaspar? What is your real name?** - I asked.
- **I am the one who is.** - He answered me and disappeared.
- **My Lord Adonai...** - I babbled as that light disappeared.

When I entered the mausoleum I noticed that the body of Jesus had disappeared, and I ran to tell the others who were still asleep in the cenacle, and we returned to the sepulchre.

- **Only the Magi or the priests would have such authority to convince the guards to leave a guarded tomb and thus remove the body. But for what purpose?** - asked Matthew.
- **With the aim of instilling terror in the Romans for having condemned an innocent man, so that disorder may materialise within this dirty, hypocritical empire, so that Israel may again have a beacon.** - Answered Caiaphas, coming out from among the foliage.
- **It was you, but you wanted his condemnation, you accused him of things he never did, and now you believe in him?** - Peter asked.
- **I always told Judas that it was better that one should**

die for all Israel, that all Israel should suffer. And this was also Jesus' message. We will never assume a messianic belief in him, but this division will be enough for the ruin of Rome. - Gamaliel explained.

- And Judas? Are you also responsible for his death? - asked Cleoppa.

- No, nor do we have any connection with Judas' death, nor do we know what really happened to him. - Caiaphas answered.

- And now, what will happen? - Matthew asked.

- You are to continue the work he has begun, and the rest will follow its own course. - Caiaphas said.

- And we will make peace, just like that, without explanations? - I asked.

- We will be invariably and seemingly adversaries, while in the name of Jesus every knee in Rome will bend and all will recognise him as messiah. Only then shall we be free. - Gamaliel replied.

- And my son's body? - Mary asked.

- It is a closely guarded secret and better that no one knows about it. - Gamaliel said.

- And when they ask us about it? - Simon asked.

- Just say that he is alive and that he lives in each one of you. - answered Caiaphas.

- But that's not a truth, and it's certainly not an answer. - Thomas retorted.

- The truth is only one point of view. Spread out in

That same day, before returning to Nazareth, Mary and I sought out Caiaphas at his house to ask him for the right to see the body of Jesus one last time. He consented and took us to the temple, to a secret place, where we were able to leave our last words there. And I remember very well everything about that night.

- **Keep it secret, that way you'll be safer. As long as we are publicly adversaries, they will never seek you here. -** Caiphas warned.
- **We will not share with anyone, not even the other disciples. -** Mary said, while I, facing her body, began to tell her everything that was in my heart.
- **My treasure, thank you for everything, thank you for brightening my days with your smile, for changing my life with your affection, for all the care you took of me, for having fallen in love with me when we were still children and never having given up on me, for having made me your world, your refuge, the place in which you rested your head. In my life your place is irreplaceable. I confess that I have no strength to go on, but I will find it in our children. I thought of calling them Judas and Joseph if they are men, or Mary and Martha if they are women. Or Joseph and**

Mary if they are a couple. Nonsense of mine, for it is all a way of not forgetting you. In any case, I thought of not giving your name to break the shackles of hatred that still surround us, to spare them any future suffering, and because your name, from today, is only yours, is only ours. Your name is, in my life, over every other name. Nothing is more precious in my heart and I hope that our children will not only look like you, but have your character, for you are the most precious possession I have found on my road. You have made me an eternal child and whenever I bathe my feet in the sea, I remember the two of us. Whenever I sink my hands in the warm sand, I remember your games. No queen was as gifted as I was, no woman was as loved as I was. Falling asleep in your arms was synonymous with safety and security. Dawning at your side was the adventure of a discovery, either you woke me up with kisses, or with the first meal, or with your perfect smile, adoring my body as your temple. No couple will ever be like the two of us. My body misses your hands, my mouth misses your mouth. Today I no longer have your arms, but I will use mine to give our children everything you gave me. This is not a goodbye, it is only a momentary separation. Soon I will be with you, either in the dust, or in paradise, it doesn't matter, as long as we are together. - my last words to Jesus.

The days that came were entirely troubled. Periods of peace, periods of persecution. Mary and I were still living in Nazareth, and I was busy raising my sons, Joseph and Judas, who were growing up well and healthy. We had the care of all, and the part of the inheritance of Jesus that Joseph of Arimathea gave us every month for our personal expenses, while the children learned their grandfather's and their father's trade.

The disciples that remained in Jerusalem were violently persecuted, mistreated, exiled, murdered; however, the more they were persecuted, more disciples emerged and, quickly, Christianity was born beyond a sect, motivating the faith of the whole empire. However, after the harsh interrogation that my brother-in-law Judas, son of Mary, suffered, Domitian summoned my two sons, seeking to know if they were heirs and successors of the Kingdom of Christ, both because of Jesus' preaching and because of the Davidic line of succession to the throne of Israel, and so we realized that it was time to escape. My sons were publicly shamed, had all their belongings taken by the empire and were dismissed not for mercy, but because Domitian was afraid that, condemning them to death, would favor new revolts in Israel, especially for being sons of Jesus.

Paul's preaching and letters contributed to a divine interpretation around Jesus, creating a series of discussions around his nature, whether he was human, whether he was divine, and for us who had lived with him, it was an affront, because only we knew how human he was, more human and merciful than anyone else.

In fact, perhaps it was this compassion and humanity, uniquely present in him, that made him seem divine. Strange, because according to his messages, the divine manifests itself when we are able to show extreme humanity towards our fellow human beings, just as today people believe him to be more special than he really was. However, the truth is that no matter what they add to his person, nothing will cause any change, because he will continue to be the best of us all. What we learn from him has nothing divine about it, he only practised and was what we were shamefully incapable of manifesting, and even though he was not divine, he was as close to God as one could get.

After Mary's funeral, already in my old age, we landed on a small beach in Gaul, when I learned that, revolted by Christian growth and the constant Jewish revolts, around the year 70, Titus had completely destroyed Jerusalem. My children were at peace and learned to fish in the little village where we lived. The message of Jesus was spreading around the world as his seeds grew under my care, and every time I got my feet wet in the sea, it was as if my husband was alive beside me.

www.ingramcontent.com/pod-product-compliance
Lightning Source LLC
Chambersburg PA
CBHW061424160726
47995CB00003B/751